Eitan
Legacy of Light

LURA RUSSELL

Published by Lazy Lizard Publishing
Knoxville, Tennessee

All characters and events in this book are fictitious.
Any resemblance to persons living or dead is strictly coincidental.

FOR MY CHILDREN

I hope you always nurture your childhood spirits so they may take you on many fantastic journeys to extraordinary places.

Chapter 1

Some call it deja vu. The unnerving thought that one has already witnessed or experienced an event in a former time. Maybe the familiar face of a friend, distinct surroundings, an unmistakable scent, or even a certain voice will trigger the sensation. Regardless of how it occurs, it is indeed an intense moment of near confusion as the mind searches through all former memories to seek out this particular event. It's an experience that anyone will remember for quite some time. For most, deja vu happens only a handful of times. For me, it happens every night in my dreams.

The breeze carried a strong sense of uncertainty. In fact, the whole atmosphere was different this time. I stiffened and listened closely for the slightest sound. While the beat of my heart was calm and steady, instinct told me to be on guard. As the breeze rustled through the leaves of the trees and softly touched my face, I was somehow comforted by the fact I was in the right place this time. The entire world began to spin around me. I closed my eyes in fear the peacefulness would end and turn to the nightmares of my usual journeys. So faint at first, I couldn't tell if the sound came from the stirring of the breeze or the audible voice of a whisper.

"Eitan. Eitan, can you hear us?"

My eyes opened, but the scenery had not changed. My head tilted and eyes narrowed as I was unsure if the voice spoke to me, or if the voice existed at all. I hesitated before answering. Spontaneously, the wind and the trees became quiet. The universe halted all movement and sound. It was transparent as it first began, and then the willow tree became a bright glowing green. I took a step back and with widened eyes reached out to touch it. The branches swirled closer to me, yet the breeze was gone.

Again the voice spoke, "Eitan."

I answered this time. "Yes, I'm listening. Where are you? Who are you?"

The voice replied, "Sweet Eitan, you have grown so much since we've seen you last."

The branches turned brighter as they stroked my cheek. They wrapped around me and pulled me closer to the massive trunk.

"Listen closely. The time is here, and you are in danger. You must sense the changes occurring in your world. These changes are happening in other worlds as well. He has found you."

"Who? Who has found me?" I asked.

The voice lowered to an almost secretive whisper, "We waited with anticipation for the day you would return to us. Your destiny is to help us. He is getting closer to finding you and he will stop at nothing."

"I don't understand," I replied.

"You MUST understand, you must learn. He wants your secret. He wants the gift you were given."

"Who?" I asked again.

My heart raced faster and my intuition took a survey of any possible exits. The branches released me and the glow of the tree darkened. The wind howled like a beast searching for prey.

The gentle voice became strong and demanding. "Hurry Eitan! You must return home now! You must always protect yourself, and remember you carry the power with you! HURRY! Kiverus knows we are speaking with you!"

I wasn't sure where I was headed, but I ran with all my speed. As I turned to glance back at the willow tree, sudden pain shot through my body as I was thrown backward to ground. I had run full speed into a tree.

I didn't remember my floor being quite as hard as it now felt. Had I rolled out of the bed? The last time I did that was six years ago. I was surprised I had not caused more damage to myself upon waking considering some of the dreams I'd had lately. I pushed myself up off the ground, but not before noticing my arms appeared somewhat larger than the day before. Those sit-ups and push-ups were finally paying off. I caught a glimpse of my full reflection in the mirror and couldn't help but acknowledge how impressive I was becoming. It was about time. All through middle school I was a puny kid. I always received good grades. Not good enough to get into an Ivy League school like my parents were hoping. But at this point in my life, college is still four years away, and high school is a perfect time for change. I can change my looks, grades, and best of all- I am turning fifteen in less than a week.

I have one best friend, Albert Eugene Tucker. Tucker wasn't exactly graced with an impressively cool name. He was, however, graced with the natural ability to absorb any scholastic information that came his way. Since our initial introduction in the third grade, his name appeared on every honor roll and every honorable mention known. I don't mind admitting I am slightly envious of his childhood fame in our small town, but I wouldn't trade our friendship for anything. As luck would have it, Tucker has been picked on by every jock from every sport in this small town of Madison.   Many long afternoons I've served my sentencing through detention from making a poor attempt to redeem Tucker's lost honor. I guess being a bodyguard isn't a wise career path for me at this point. I'm definitely becoming a greater challenge for them lately though. I've grown a full ten inches and twenty pounds over last summer vacation. The amount of whispering in the halls has doubled over the last few weeks, and I like to believe they are discussing my physique as I walk by. It's interesting how people will stare and whisper in one breath when they think you *aren't* looking, and then smile with the sweetest of intentions when you *do* look at them.

This town is fairly small. Madison is an upper middle class suburb with beautiful homes and every street with a sidewalk. My house is a gray and white brick house. It's a charming home, but somehow it still seems so ordinary and plain compared to some of the other houses. There are two houses between Tucker's and mine. We live two blocks from the school, so we usually walk. Not to count the advantages of maybe catching Kallie on her way to school.

Kallie Thompson is my neighbor. We grew up living next to each other, but have never had a conversation longer than four minutes. Kallie is by far the most beautiful girl at Madison High School. Although she's never shown interest in me before, this is the year for change, and I've not given up hope just yet.

My daydreaming was interrupted by the doorbell. It was Tucker. By the impatient look he had, I was running late. I scrambled to finish getting dressed and darted out the door. Mom and Dad were usually gone to work by the time I leave for school so we had our family interaction time during dinner. Tucker, with his wide grin, was almost bouncing as we walked. We were going to be assigned science projects today. I didn't see a reason to get excited. Tucker, on the other hand, leaped for joy at every chance to visit the public library after school hours.

"Ethan!" Tucker spoke with an elated tone. "I talked to Mrs. Gibbs yesterday. She said we're going to be able to choose our own project partners."

Sounding as if there was a down side to his previous statement, he said, "Of course I'd love for us to work together. Um, I just don't want to do all the work alone again."

"Tucker! I helped. I helped a lot!" I insisted.

"We agreed to formulate a teeth-whitening product from household materials which could be marketable in today's society. You chose to help by brushing your teeth every morning," Tucker said with irritation.

"Yeah, but I used *our* products. Someone had to test them." I'm sure my smirk gave away the fact I was being sarcastic.

Tucker didn't seem amused. "Someone also had to do the research, lab work, creation of the products, and the REPORT. Brushing your teeth in the name of science seems a little vain considering the grand scheme of the project."

The walk to school was only two blocks away. Yet today with the way Tucker rambled on, it seemed like miles. He never slowed his speech for a minute. You would have thought as intelligent as he was, he would have enough perception to notice I wasn't listening. I was, however, trying to avoiding tripping over myself from wondering if Kallie was somewhere behind us.

I happened to notice Dane Ivey's house as we walked by. I'm not really sure who wouldn't notice it. It was beautiful. It was the biggest house in the neighborhood, and everything looked completely perfect. Its biggest flaw was it had the neighborhood's most prominent jerk living in it. Dane Ivey was every teenage boy's nightmare. He was flawless in appearance and beyond compare when it came to any sports. Just the mention of his name sent the girls into a frenzy of giggling and primping.

The closer we got to school, the sound of the school buses further toned out Tucker's chattering. A small crowd gathered in the front parking lot of the school. As we got closer, I saw Dane. Evidently, his parents bought him a new car. We all grew up in this small town together. Year after year, Dane's parents set the bar high for any birthday events, gatherings, or presents following his. Unfortunately, my birthday fell one week after his. In my younger years, this usually meant other kids' parents were either too tired or broke after Dane's party to allow them to come to mine.

I guess it would have been too much to ask if Tucker and I just walked right past unnoticed.

"Moron!"

I don't think Tucker had even taken survey of his surroundings since we left the house.

"Hey nerd goggles, I'm talking to you!"

His sudden silence made it obvious that he realized the weekly assault was about to begin. I felt partly responsible this morning. I was running late due to my dreaming escapade. We recently learned to avoid Dane by simply arriving at the school five minutes earlier each day. It wasn't Tucker's fault. I guess he was just an easy target.

I spoke the words before the thought even processed in my mind. "How bout you shut up and just keep showin' off that pretty car Mommy and Daddy bought you!"

Did those words seriously come out of my mouth? No. Surely it was just a thought. The firm push on my back told me the words indeed made their way out of my mouth. To make the situation even worse, Kallie had been only a few steps behind us.

"You sure you wanna play Captain Save-A-Nerd today, Ethan?" Dane taunted.

"Hey, I'm not looking for trouble. Just lay off a little. This has been going on every week since the third grade. What's the point? We all know you can beat him up."

"Yea, but the question is how much damage can I do to you?"

And with his next breath, Dane put his hands on my chest and shoved me back into Tucker. Tucker, as nervous as he was, lost his footing and still managed to fall to the ground. I, on the other hand, now stood nose to nose with Dane. I was pretty sure I'd make a fool out of myself if a fight actually started. Fortunately, Shelby James, loving the smell of power and control, stepped in to gather a better sniff. A soft breath whispered to the both of us.

"As sexy as a fight would be, we are going to be late for class. Come on Dane, you can always have some fun later."

Dane and Shelby had flirted with each other for years. They recently decided to take their relationship public. Honestly, I'm still confused as to why Shelby was one of Kallie's best friends. Shelby was the female version of Dane. They deserved each other to say the least. She was gorgeous and probably everything every girl in school strived to be. In my opinion, she was just a little too much glitter.

Dane gave me a glare suggesting this discussion wasn't over. Shelby took his hand and led him into the school. I turned and held out my hand to help Tucker up off the ground. Stumbling and shaking, he grabbed my arm.

"I can't believe you just did that, Ethan," he said.

I honestly couldn't believe I did either. Every aspiring bully in the school picked on Tucker for years. I've been in many fights trying to defend my friend, but this by far would have been my paramount event. I was almost lost in thoughts when I turned and noticed Kallie still standing there. She handed me a book.

"You dropped this. You... you might need it," she said softly.

She smiled when she spoke to me, first with her eyes and then her mouth. I was frozen. My mouth became uncomfortably dry.

"Are you ok?" she asked.

"I'm fine. I just, you, um...thanks," I stuttered like a fool.

She giggled a little and then walked away. I watched her walk, and it was as if the sunlight shone directly and solely on her. Everything else ceased to exist.

"Ethan! Dude, are you still on the planet? Were you NOT here when you just called out Dane Ivey? What's wrong with you?" Tucker's panic button had certainly been pushed.

"Nothing is wrong. Life is perfect."

I probably sounded so lame, but I didn't care. Life *did* seem perfect.

The rest of the day was uneventful to say the least. It was Wednesday. Wednesday was like any other day with one exception. My parents had long ago started the tradition of inviting Tucker over for dinner on Wednesdays. I could smell it the moment we walked through the door. My mom cooked some of the best homemade meals. She was naturally a wonderful cook. For some reason, she felt the need to exhibit these skills on a weekly basis. It was certainly worth the required compliments in order to gorge over a delicious feast with friends.

"Hello, boys. How was school today?"

It was a rhetorical question. She was so consumed with creating her masterpiece, we could have said we made a mistake in chemistry class and brought the entire school to its melting point, and would not have gotten so much as an eyebrow raised in return.

"Same stuff, another day," I said as I kissed her on the cheek.

"And Tucker? How about your day?"

Tucker began to utter something when water began to over boil onto the stove.

"Shoot! You boys go on upstairs and play."

We hadn't "played" in years. I suppose she still pictured me as her little boy. Although when it was time to do chores, I was certainly considered all grown up.

"I'll call you when dinner is ready. Oh! And Tucker, I spoke with your parents and they are going to join us for dinner tonight."

I thoroughly enjoyed when Tucker's parents came to visit for dinner. Despite the fact our dads sat for hours planning our future colleges, careers, and lives, Tucker's mom would always bring mouthwatering desserts. My mind was filled with all the delicious desserts from the recent past.

Tucker was obviously still consumed with planning our science project. As we topped the stairs, I heard him mumbling something about refraction of light. It sounded way too intense to even begin an attempt to understand. Besides, at this point, all I could think about was Kallie and her beautiful smile.

Between my daydreaming, video games, and the rambling of a friend, time passed quickly and dinner was ready. Tucker's parents, Judy and Alan, had just arrived, and I could already hear my dad and Alan determining the topic of our dinner conversation.

"Mike, let's try to give Ethan a break tonight. You've been awful hard on him lately," my mom said in attempts to intervene on my behalf.

"Sherry, kids don't become people who impact the world by having parents who take it easy on them," he said with a condescending tone.

"True. True," Alan agreed in return.

Mom became even more frustrated. "Come on Judy; let's put your pie in the fridge."

Tucker and I were called to dinner. Our eyes met, and it was apparent we both felt the same way about the upcoming events. We agreed to each other that remaining in control and staying reserved were the best options, and then we proceeded down the stairs. Wonderful scents filled the air and our mouths naturally watered with anticipation.

I wish I could have said the same for my ears, but my dad started almost immediately.

"So report cards come out in just another week or so, don't they? How do you think you'll do, son?" he asked.

"All right, I suppose," I said with hesitation.

"Suppose?" he asked as he chewed. "Better keep those grades up if you are going to try out for the football team soon! You already missed tryouts this summer. Guess the best you can hope for is they'll let you come to practices and maybe bench it out the rest of the year."

My thoughts on the subject were only going to intensify the mood, and I probably should've just kept them to myself. Instead, "I'm not sure I want to play…"

"What do you mean "not sure"? Ethan, I've told you son. It's time your grades reached their ultimate potential, and you *are* going to follow in our family tradition," he said, as everyone prepared for the next statement, "I played ball, Grandpa played ball, his father played ball. As far back as we know, our entire legacy derived from ball playing men that attended some of the top leading universities in this country! In fact-"

My mother attempted to distract him. She interrupted, "Mike, speaking of football, did you remember to schedule the DVR for Sunday's game?"

Her ploy worked. "Yes Sherry, of course I did."

Judy successfully assisted, "Albert, did you know that your packages came in the mail from the science and technology store?"

Oblivious to the direction his mom was leading the conversation, Tucker became ecstatic, "Already! I wasn't expecting them for at least another two days!"

Tucker, now lost in his own world, "Ethan, you are going to love these new kits that I ordered! I will be able to determine the chemical makeup of-"

"See Ethan," my dad said as he interrupted Tucker, "That's just what I'm talking about. Tucker here, has a game plan, and he's striving for every yard."

Alan decided to voice his opinion, "I'm only trying to encourage you Ethan, but Albert has already turned in several applications for scholarships. Have you begun to think about where you might want to continue your education? It's always smart to have a plan," Alan gently prompted.

"Um. Yeah, I've thought about it. I just need to make the time to request some information, and stuff," I knew the answer better be satisfying to my dad.

"Well, that's great to know, Ethan," my dad said with real surprise. "I'm really impressed to hear you say that, son. I know sometimes I push you a little, but I honestly just want extraordinary things for your future. It's tough coming from a small town. Trust me, I know. If you don't fight your way to the top, you'll always just be looked at as an ordinary kid from the little town of Madison."

"You use the word *ordinary* like it's a curse or something," I muttered.

"It is. I mean..." he nodded toward Alan in reassurance the reference didn't pertain to him or Tucker, "...there's always a place in the world for *ordinary* people, someone has to do it. I just sense there's more inside of you, Ethan. I saw it the first time I looked into your eyes. You have the potential to be so much more than *just* ordinary."

My recent dreams confirmed what he said, but it just wasn't in the way he was describing. I knew I was created for a greater purpose. I just couldn't figure out what the purpose might be.

We finished our dinner with much enlightening topics, but the words lingered in my mind. I wanted to stand out. I wanted to shine and become someone my parents would love to brag about. I was pretty sure, however, it wasn't going to happen on their terms.

Chapter 2

I've spent a lot of time being uncertain about things. Uncertain about the man I would one day become. Uncertain why people behave the way they do. Uncertain, in fact, of the whole universe and the way it rules itself. I suppose this is fairly normal considering the greatest of minds are still clueless in such areas. Here lately though, I feel quite uncertain about much more. I know I am turning fifteen next week, but there is more to it. It's more than just physical changes I feel. It's almost as if the rest of my life is dependent on everything that happens today. It feels as if something greater is calling my name and trying to lead me. As to where, I have no idea. That seems to be the issue that is plaguing my mind and soul.

I continue to have these dreams and it's as if they are trying to guide me, to let me in on some secret. They have been very confusing, frustrating, and even distressing. As I lie here awake, attempting to make sense of them, my heart feels as though it is going to literally thump out of my chest.

I was standing in the garden again. I like the dreams that occur here, they usually feel so peaceful. Everything appears to have exquisite shades of blues and greens. When things are tranquil here, its brilliance is almost heavenly. There is a slight breeze that blows in harmony with the surrounding nature. A beckoning light exists beyond some trees in the short distance that I haven't been able to explore yet. From the very first time my dreams brought me to this place, it has felt like home.

My curiosity is drawn to the majestic willow tree that demands my attention upon arrival. The wind blows in such a way it sounds like wailing. The leaves on the trees sound as if someone is grabbing them by the trunk and shaking a baby's rattle.

The recently familiar voice acknowledged my presence.

"Eitan.   We are so happy you have returned here once again. We have something to show you this time."

A small pool of water gathered at the base of the trunk. An image began to form, but the ripples made it hard to see clearly. I moved a little closer. As the ripples slowed, I saw the image of a man. Stress caused visible strain around his intense blue eyes. His brow was broad and ingrained with similar lines of tension. Standing out the most, was his notably strong jaw line. Being so distinguished, it drew immediate attention to the seriousness of his mouth. He spoke to me.

"Hello Eitan. You must have many questions."

"Why do you keep calling me Eitan? My name is *Ethan*. Perhaps you have mistaken me for someone else."

The man answered, "We know who you are, and be assured there is no mistake. Your name was chosen before you were born into existence. You were named Eitan, and you have always been Eitan. We have been awaiting your return."

"I don't understand. Why me?" I asked.

"Because you were chosen long before you were born, and you have the mark that confirms this choosing. You carry the name of nobility within your blood, and because you carry a gift, a power that is vital to the universes. All of creation is dependent upon your success."

Surprised by the list of attributes I was given, I replied, "That's a lot of responsibility for a kid, don't you think?"

The man answered, "You will learn, you *must* learn. Kiverus has been searching intently for you nearly fifteen years. You have something he wants, and he will stop at nothing to take it from you. Listen closely. He knows where you are, in this world and in yours. You *are* in danger. I'm sorry to hasten your leave, but you must go now."

"How do I-" I was interrupted.

"QUICKLY! Run, Eitan! Pay attention to the world around you. Do not put yourself in danger. And when the time is right, you will find us again. We will help you, and you will help us. You will restore balance to all the worlds."

A powerful clap of thunder shook the earth beneath my feet. Gusts of strong wind forced me to lose my footing. The man's reflection had turned to images of terrifying beings wearing black shrouds. I couldn't see their faces. The vibrations of the earth caused the water to ripple again. The ones wearing shrouds were capturing people and imprisoning them. There were men, women, and children alike. I heard their faint cries and screaming for help as the water vanished back into the ground. Almost as loud as the thunder, there came a commanding voice.

"LEAVE NOW AND RETURN HOME!"

And just like with every other dream, this one ended with me running. Not sure where I was headed, but certain it was as fast as I could go.

As I awoke, I lay there in bed wondering. Wondering if it is normal for people to have such unusual dreams. Wondering if it is normal for dreams to feel so real. I can only imagine a psychologist would love the opportunity to penetrate into the greatest depths of my mind. I'm sure the experience would contribute to an extremely tedious project. Speaking of projects, the sunlight began to invade the darkness in my room, and I was sure Tucker and all his enthusiasm would be here soon.

I was dressed and ready to go long before the doorbell sounded this morning. It was going to be hard to distract my thoughts from anything other than my dream. I felt as though something was wrong. Not just within myself but within all realms of life. It was a very unsettling aura that made me consider the reality of the foretold prophecy. The walk to school was a little quieter than usual.

"Is something bothering you, Ethan?" Tucker asked.

I attempted to gather my thoughts and determine if this was something worth sharing or if I would just come across as deranged.

Tucker tried again, "We've been friends for as long as I can remember. I can tell something is wrong. If you don't want to talk about it, that's fine. I think you would feel better if you did."

"Tucker, it's not that I don't want to tell you, I'm just not sure you will be able to relate. See, I had this dream last night, and it's left me with an overwhelming eerie vibe this morning," I replied.

"I've had bad dreams before. Why wouldn't I understand?" Tucker adjusted his glasses.

"Dude, it wasn't *just* a bad dream. It was *real*. I mean, it seemed real. Very real. I was told things that- never mind. I guess a dream is a dream, good or bad. Let's talk about something else and maybe get my mind back to the here and now."

Tucker changed subjects. "Okay. So did you finish your summary review on Hamlet?"

Panic shot through me, "Crap! I left it on my desk by the printer. You go on, and I'll get it and catch up to you, hopefully before the first bell."

Still tired from all of the running I did last night, my legs felt as though they might turn to jelly before I made it home. I saw Kallie and Shelby about three houses away.

"Morning, Kallie," I managed to huff out as I ran by.

She smiled and replied, "Good morning, Ethan."

Shelby shouted a sarcastic comment as my nose indulged the wonderful scent of Kallie's perfume.

I made it home, grabbed my papers, and began the race back to school. The school was in sight when my body had had enough. Late or not, my pace became a mild walk. As my breathing slowed back to normal, the uncanny atmosphere returned also. It grew stronger the closer I got to the school. The wind blew as if something evil controlled the air.

The first bell rang as I crossed the street and headed up the steps to the front entrance. I made it up four steps when I had to stop. Not because of exhaustion, but because I felt something behind me. I stopped and looked to see what it was. There was nothing. In fact, the road was unusually quiet, and most kids were already inside the school. The only noise came from a homeless man pushing a cart across the street. He struggled to move the cart from the road to the sidewalk. At that moment, I realized how strange it was.

Not that one area of town is preferred for the homeless over others, but it was rare to see him considering the upper class neighborhood we were in. He sensed that I was watching him because he froze and halted all movement. There was this strange attraction to continue to watch him, but I was running late and couldn't afford another tardy slip.

I turned my eyes and finished my way up the stairs when a flash of light blinded me. It came from his direction. When I turned back to look at him again, he stood erect with his head slightly bowed toward the ground. Something shiny was under his long coat near his beltline on the right side. Maybe it had just caught the reflection of the sunlight and stunned me for a moment. I wasn't going to dwell on it. My eyes lifted from the object back to his face and I noticed he stared intently back at me. He was an older man whose skin obviously aged with time. Judging by his dark skin, he must have spent a lot of time in the sun. His beard was overgrown. It matched the rest of his attire and needed some serious grooming. His eyes appeared to be hollow or something. A bizarre color of bluish gray, made them seem as if they were looking into my soul. The man was motionless.

Visions and thoughts from my dream came flooding back. I turned and quickly made my way up the stairs and into the door. Once inside, I resolved to take a last look, but like a ghost, he vanished. It was as if he was never there. Even the shopping cart and all of its contents were gone. The unsettling feelings I had all morning, just doubled in intensity.

I made my way down the long halls of the school. People who were trying to make it to class on time were pushing and being pushed in return. Excitement got louder as I neared my locker. There was a large crowd of kids laughing and taunting. Papers were flying everywhere. Some of the kids parted as I pushed through to my locker. I saw Dane's head in the center of all the commotion. To my dismay, I saw Tucker lifted into the air and slammed onto a locker.

"Put the crybaby to bed in the locker, Dane!" Rodney Garrett shouted above the crowd. Rodney had been Dane's accomplice since the seventh grade when he had his fourteen-inch growth

spurt. Like Dane, Rodney was active in every sport. He wasn't
quite as good looking as Dane, but was still considered high
status on the girls' scale of boyfriend material.

Rodney opened Tucker's locker. Just as I made my way
forward to the big show himself, Mr. Neils came flying through the
crowd and in one swift move had Dane backed up to the locker
and Tucker safely on the ground. For once, I was glad to see Mr.
Neils. I was impressed he moved so quickly considering he was
just an Algebra teacher.

"Everyone get to your classrooms! Now!" Mr. Neils offered no
suggestions, it was definitely a command. "Dane, you go straight
to Mr. Clinton's office."

The path to my locker quickly cleared. Tucker's eyes were
wide and sweat drops of panic slid down his cheeks.

"Are you ok?" I asked.

Tucker replied with a very unconvincing tone, "Yeah, man."

"I'm sorry," I said.

"For what?" He asked.

"If I had been here, maybe it wouldn't have gone that far."

Tucker brushed himself off, "Stop being ridiculous. I'm Dane's
toy and have been for years. He isn't going to leave me alone just
because you demand it. You can't keep trying to save me from
him. You'll just end up getting hurt yourself."

"Thanks for the vote of confidence, Bro," I said.

His opinion slightly aggravated me. Just because Dane
successfully shoved more kids into lockers than any previously

known bully, and was the number one reason kids would fake being sick or just flat out skip school, didn't mean I would automatically lose if I fought him. I mean after all, I had grown quite a bit this last summer and have been completely dedicated to working out. I think the problem was simply that everyone was just too scared to try. I was anything but scared of Dane. Here lately, I had much more to be concerned about than some jock bully thinking he could stomp me.

"Come on, Tucker, let's get to class," I said.

Chapter 3

To read or not to read, was not the question. In spite of the fact that studying Hamlet sucked, I actually related to him just a little. Having strange dreams that turned out to be reality, wondering what went on around him, who he could trust, and the question of whether these events brought him to the point of insanity or if it was all just for show. Sometimes, I felt as though I was going crazy myself. My daydreaming in class was as frequent as my dreaming at night. I should've been writing my analysis on Hamlet's ramblings, yet all I could think about was my dream.

As much as I'd like to convince myself it was just a dream, everything inside of me, everything around me, told me differently. My encounter with the homeless man this morning left me more anxious than usual. I caught myself repeatedly looking out the window in hopes that I would catch another glimpse of the stranger. I'm not sure if it would have made me feel better or worse. I was consumed with wondering how he managed to disappear so quickly. Maybe if I saw him again, I'd be relieved in knowing that it wasn't all in my mind. I desperately needed confirmation in distinguishing between imaginary and reality.

Saving me from further frustration, the final bell of the day rang. Tucker's locker sat right next to mine, making it our regular meeting place at the end of the day. Generally, we walked home together, but today we had other plans. Tucker insisted upon getting to the public library in order to have first choice of available books. We were assigned the glorious task of attempting to explain the phenomenon known as green flashes. Evidently, if you look closely at a sunset, or sunrise, there is a brief moment in which a mysterious green light will appear right at the top of the sun. I've heard of this before, but considering it has yet to be reasonably explained, I doubt that I would find a logical conclusion to its existence. On the other hand, I have faith in Tucker. He has a deep eagerness to learn about things that are unexplainable. He tends to come up with very thought out, usually long, but extremely logical explanations to the unknown.

We set up camp at a table towards the front of the library. Within thirty minutes of being there, Tucker retreated back to the table with armfuls of books. I guess it was promising he actually found some helpful information. My lacking attention immediately changed to intense as I noticed Kallie walking through the door with Shelby and Megan. Without pausing in their conversation or lowering their voices as they entered, Shelby and Megan giggled as their presence became known throughout the library. Kallie smiled at me as she walked by. I almost turned around to make sure she wasn't looking at someone else, but I didn't want to look stupid. I returned the smile with a, not so cool, nod of the head. I attempted to push down any obvious emotions that would give the impression I was about to explode with excitement on the inside. It was at this moment I actually examined the layout of the library for the first time. I had to find a reason to approach her and make conversation. Her smile was definitely a huge sign my hopes weren't completely in vain.

I tried to help Tucker find the research information he was looking for in the massive stack of books, but I honestly couldn't concentrate. Kallie got up from her table and walked toward the shelves. The library was actually very large despite the fact it was located in such a small town. It felt awkward as I followed her up and down the rows trying to go unnoticed. I concealed myself with a small section of empty shelves where I got a good glimpse of her. She was flawless in every way. Even the way she took and replaced the books seemed graceful. Her hair was brown, but simply saying *brown* didn't give it justice. I would have to describe it with loose, long curls that displayed every shade from honey and caramel to toffee. Her body was very slender and shapely. Every curve perfected her shape and size. As I stood there secretly watching her every move, I wondered what it would be like to hold her. Her eyes were a delicate shade of green that may have been overlooked by anyone who didn't take close notice. The only notable sign of makeup was her lip gloss. At that moment, my stealth-like ninja skills showed by leaning a little too far and knocking a book off the shelf. Of course it caught her off guard, and she turned to look right at me through the empty section of the shelving. I practically melted with embarrassment. She took the book that was in her hand and walked toward me.

The scent of warm vanilla and the large metal shelving was the only thing separating us.

"Ethan?" she whispered quietly.

"Yeah. Hi Kallie," I answered.

"Are you here working on your science project?" she asked.

I thought before answering, "Um, yeah, I'm not being very productive, though."

She snickered a little under her breath, "Perhaps if you were in the section with the science material instead of the romance novels you'd find something a little more useful?"

I glanced around and realized how out of place I appeared in the one area of the library that was most commonly visited by females. I silently laughed at myself over how silly I looked.

"I suppose I should save the cheesy love and drama material for another day, huh?" I mumbled.

"Probably," she said as she smiled and made her way back to the table. Her walk was perfection. I couldn't help but notice her long and slender legs made her skirt look even shorter.

Deciding to return to my own table, a familiar yet strange feeling overwhelmed me. An overpowering urge to go deeper into the maze of book rows beckoned to me. I had never really been to the back section of the library, so I was clueless as to what was even there. It was if someone was watching me, but I didn't see anyone. I found myself constantly looking behind, through the shelves, and around the corners. It became frightening, like I was being stalked. I heard someone breathing. I slowly walked closer to where the noise came from when a faint drumming sound joined the quietness. It kept perfect rhythm with my pounding heart, and got louder with every step. The entire main area of the library was out of view. A sudden gust of air, which was impossible considering there weren't any fans or vents, blew across my body. I wondered if it was the presence of a ghost or something. The windy sounds became louder. Reminding me of the intense likeness of my dreams, I wanted to run. Surely someone would hear all of this and come to see what was going on, but no one did. The air ruffled through my hair again. I inched back towards the wall when a violent burst of air knocked several books onto the floor at my feet. I knew the draft wasn't my imagination when I looked down and saw it flipping through the pages of the books. And then, just as quickly as it began, it ended. It just stopped. The wind, the drumming, all noises and movement ceased.

What was going on? This was crazy. The only thing I knew for sure was it was *not* my imagination. This somehow related to my dreams. The realness of danger surrounded me. Utter fear built inside of me. If I tried to tell anyone, they would think I had lost my mind. I put the books back where they belonged, and then Tucker came around the corner startling me.

"There you are! Ethan, what are you doing? I've been looking everywhere for you."

"I... really don't know. I don't know what I'm doing," I answered.

"Well come on, man. We've got to get home, and I've got to start looking some things up on the Internet," Tucker said.

"Okay, I'm coming."

I don't think he sensed any abnormality in my voice. I picked up the final book and noticed how odd and out of place it looked. It was very old. I searched both the front and binding, but couldn't find a title. The pages were worn and looked faded with time. They were hand written with hand drawn pictures. I moved my finger across the front and a layer of dust came up with it. Something almost magnetic pulled me to this book. A strange and raised emblem appeared on the front. Part of the image was a sun, but the other half was too flattened and faded to see.

"Ethan?" Tucker sounded frustrated.

We gathered our things, the books Tucker wanted, and headed to check out.

Mrs. Warren, the librarian, greeted us with a smile, "Well hello, Mr. Tucker. How are we doing today?"

"Pretty good, Mrs. Warren. I think I found most of what I need. Although, I wouldn't mind coming back another day to double check," Tucker said as he winked at Mrs. Warren.

I couldn't help but roll my eyes and chuckle. Mrs. Warren had been the librarian here for at least 40 years before we were even born. She fit the typical librarian profile, old, gray hair, glasses, and very stern. Except when Tucker was around, and then she went from stern to pleasant. It was peculiar as to why he would seemingly flirt with this lady. Her husband had died a few years ago, and she distanced herself from people for some time after. Tucker, if nothing else, consistently brightened her day.

She placed her hand on top of his, "I've ordered something special for you. It should be here at the first of the week."

Like a schoolgirl Tucker blushed, "I can't wait! I just love surprises."

"Excuse me. Mrs. Warren? I wonder if you could tell me more about this book." I placed the book on the counter.

"Well, Ethan, honestly I've never seen this book before." She took a quick glance at the inside of the front and back covers.

"There aren't even any of the old cards we used to sign the books out with. It's obviously been here a while, and it doesn't have a barcode. Where did you find this book?"

I hesitated to answer, "In the back. I was in the back when it… when… I stumbled across it."

"Ethan, sweetheart, if you have an interest in it, just take it with you," she said.

Uncomfortable about taking it, I hesitated, "Oh, I don't want to-"

She interrupted, "It's fine, honey. Honestly." She laughed a little, "I'm sure where ever it came from, it has found its way to you for a reason."

I still wasn't sure I wanted to take the book. I couldn't understand the words that were in it. And even though the pictures looked interesting, some of them were too faded to even see. I slipped the book into my backpack anyway as Tucker and Mrs. Warren finished their discussion.

A cold chill started at my toes and climbed to the top of my head. It was so cold it nearly paralyzed me. Instinctively, my head searched for warmth and turned toward the large window. There was a man looking at the magazine racks. He caught my attention because he seemed so out of place. The library was full of teenagers working on their class projects, and mothers with small children doing the weekly pick up for bedtime stories. And there stood this sharply dressed man. He turned at an angle just enough that I couldn't see his face. I examined him from top to bottom. He was tall, lanky, and his shoes were overly shiny and expensive. His shirt and pants were unusually straight. His head was bald and very smooth. His hands were incredibly large with long slender fingers, and his cuff links were golden along with his watch and ring. I hadn't been watching him for very long, but he never turned a page. In fact, he was motionless. I wasn't sure he was breathing.

Starring at the man made me uncomfortable, and I shifted my attention back to Tucker to see what was taking so long. At that moment, I witnessed the same bright flash that had almost blinded me earlier that morning. Within an instant, the man completely faced me and intently focused on me as though he could read my mind. His eyes were the same hollow, bluish gray as the homeless man's eyes. His face was pale white, and his lips had a strange hint of red. He appeared much taller now than he did when his back was turned. His spider-like fingers reached for the golden object that hung from his pocket. It must have been what caught my eye, but what was it?

Tucker's hand on my back startled me and I actually jumped a little.

"Hey dude, why so jumpy? It's time to go," he said.

"Sorry. I guess I was just distracted by that man over by the magazines," I answered.

Tucker glanced toward the window, "What man?"

I looked back, and just like earlier today, he was gone. My face turned as white as a sheet.

"He was just there," I said with distress.

"You okay Ethan? You've been acting really strange the last couple of days. Come on, maybe it's the library's smart air getting to you. Let's get out of here," Tucker suggested.

I was distracted all the way home. Tucker tried to play it off and help me forget whatever he thought bothered me, but it simply didn't work. He should have known by now I preferred to keep my troubles and thoughts to myself. Normally, this worked out well for our friendship. But this time, I honestly would have preferred to share with him. On the other hand, I'm sure it would have sent Tucker into a raging frenzy of either trying to psychoanalyze me or into a mystery investigation of great proportions. Either way, loss of sleep and peace for the both of us would have been the result. It was probably best to keep this one to myself.

Tucker had a concerned tone in his voice, "Call me later. You know, if you decide you want to talk or anything."

"Thanks, Tuck. I'm just going to grab some left over food and head to my room. Maybe I'll start this homework and attempt to get some sleep later. That way I won't make us late in the morning."

I tried to produce a reassuring smile to let him know I was okay.

"All right Ethan. Have a good night," Tucker said as he walked on.

I picked up my backpack and went into the house. My mom was finishing up the dishes.

"Hi sweetie! Did you find what you needed at the library?"

"Yeah, and then some."

She sensed the sarcasm in my tone. "What do you mean?" she asked.

"Nothing, sorry. It's just been a long day. If you don't care, I'm going to take dinner to my room tonight and study," I said.

"That's fine. I figured you would, so I fixed you a plate and put it in the microwave," she said.

"Thanks, Mom."

"No problem, sweetie. You're my growing boy. Be sure to eat all your veggies tonight, helps the brain power." She winked as she chuckled to herself. She was cute when she'd say something that would make her laugh at herself.

I kissed her on the cheek and as I headed out of the kitchen. I heard my dad watching a ball game in the living room.

"Hey, Dad," I said as I passed by him to the stairs.

"Hey Ethan! Missed you at dinner tonight. Just isn't the same without you. Have you thought any more about maybe trying out for the football team this year?" he asked.

I reluctantly continued, "No, not really. Like I said, I just don't get along with some of those guys and I think it would be awkward to try to play on the same team with them."

Unaffected by my thoughts, he said, "It'd be a great way to get a scholarship. Not to count, it would push you to keep your grades up. But, I'll lay off of it tonight. It just excites me to see you excelling in school the way you have the last year or so. I may not tell you often, but I *am* proud of you!"

"Thanks, Dad," I lifted my plate a little, and nodded my head. "I'm going to go get started studying now. Go Cowboys!" I said as I left the room.

I heard my dad talking to the referees through the television. I knew far too well he could get fiercely passionate over something as simple as a football game. My mom would go sit by him on the couch and help cheer on whatever team he was rooting for. Hopefully, the outcome of the game would go his way and she'd end up having a good night as well. If she wasn't so fortunate, she'd have a night of listening to him fuss in his sleep about everyone from players, to coaches, to referees, and even announcers.

I tossed my backpack on the bed and sat down at my desk to eat. Home fried chicken, mashed potatoes, corn, okra, and biscuits all adorned my plate. A gentle breeze blew my curtains into the air. It didn't take long before I was stuffed. I usually had some music playing or some background noise, but tonight I was enjoying listening to the breeze. All of a sudden, I remembered the book from the library and the strangeness of how I found it. Curiosity quickly took over.

I shuffled through the things in my backpack until I found it. I sat it down on the desk in front of me, and examined the front of the book a little closer than I had earlier. The emblem was so intriguing. I grabbed a dirty shirt and finished wiping the dust off of it. I could now see there were five symbols centered under the emblem. They looked like a form of ancient letters or writing. The book became even more mysterious and confusing when I looked inside. The writing was in the same style of ancient letters that were used on the cover. There were tons of illustrations, none of which made any sense without the accompanying words. Then I came to a page that left me breathless. It was a drawing of a man. But not just *any* man. It was the man from my dream. It was the man whose face appeared in the water under the willow tree. There were other people in the book as well, but I couldn't move beyond the fact of knowing that this book somehow connected to my dreams. If anyone knew how to find out what these writings meant, it would be Tucker.

I heard someone talking outside the window. As I put the book back into my backpack, I recognized the voice. It was Kallie. I moved closer to the window so I could hear her, but stayed low enough down so she wouldn't see me.

"OMG Kallie! You have GOT to be kidding me! Please tell me you aren't being serious," Shelby spoke with a stern commanding tone.

"Well, maybe. I don't know. It was just a thought."

"I'll tell ya what you need to do. You need to get your mind off of this! I expect you to be ready by eight o'clock sharp tomorrow night! You *ARE* going to Dane's party with us. It is just what the doctor ordered. I'm sure you'll find someone there that'll be more than willing to give you better things to think about."

"Shelby-"

"Nope nope nope! No excuses, Missy. In fact, I'll be here by seven to help you get dressed. You are going to look so hot and sexy!" Shelby exclaimed.

Kallie's unsure words instantly turned to confidence. "Can I borrow that green top of yours that I like so much? You know I look better in it than you do anyway."

Shelby laughed, "Of course you can! And yes, you do look great in it! Okay, so I'll see you in the morning on the way to school. I can't wait…. This is going to be a blast!"

"Okay, Shelby. Have a good night," Kallie said as she hugged Shelby.

I peeked up over the bottom of the window sill just in time to watch Kallie walk up her front steps and go inside. Gazing into the stillness of the night, I thought about how awesome Kallie looked in anything and everything. It didn't have to be green. My thoughts were cut short when her bedroom light came on. Her curtains were open and I saw her clearly. She walked over to her full-length mirror and took different pairs of jeans from her closet and held them up to her. She turned to the front, back, and even the side. She had her phone and must have been texting someone. I decided it was time for me to close my curtains and try to catch up on some sleep tonight. After all, I had invaded enough of her privacy for the day. No need to push my luck.

I lay down in bed wondering what events were in store for me. I was beginning to dread the act of sleeping. It used to be my favorite hobby. Not so much anymore. I remembered the homeless man and the man at the library and how their eyes envisioned my entire being. There was an equal emotion of fear and exhaustion inside of me. I wondered which would win my thoughts tonight as I drifted off.

Chapter 4

Kallie closely examined herself as she tried on different pairs of jeans. It amazed her how one brand of jeans would make the curves appear much smaller while others would emphasize them. She knew she looked great in all of them, but still felt there was a perfect pair for each occasion.

"Ya know, I may have an old pair in my closet that would look stunning on you. You can help yourself if you want," her mom said with a smile.

Kallie took a step back and saw her mom leaning in the doorway.

"How long have you been standing there?" Kallie asked with an embarrassed tone.

"Long enough to see you are having trouble finding some jeans," her mom replied.

"Can we go look in your closet *now?* I need them for tomorrow night," Kallie insisted.

"Sure baby, come on."

Kallie wasn't sure what prompted her mom to come upstairs, but she was glad she did. Her mom led the way back downstairs to the bedroom. She looked a little thinner than she had the last time Kallie noticed. She started to say something, but decided it wasn't the time to have that conversation again. She'd been worried about her mom the last few years. And it seemed as though she slipped into a new level of depression. Thinking it would help, she had recently been on mission to find her mom a boyfriend. Needless to say, it was an unsuccessful quest.

There was never any question as to where Kallie got her beautiful looks. Anna was the mom that would make teenage boys drool, still being young herself. On the morning of her last birthday, she found her first gray hair. She stayed devastated for weeks. She drove Kallie crazy walking around the house mumbling things about only being 32 and having gray hair. Anna was tall and slender with a very charming demeanor. Kallie never understood why her mom insisted on being alone.

Kallie hardly remembered her father. The things she did remember were stories that were told while looking through old photos with her mom. She was seven years old the last time she saw him. Half of her life had now been spent without him. Still, she missed him. She missed the family that she saw in the pictures, and she missed the obvious joy displayed on her mom's face before he was gone. Kallie enjoyed thinking about the times she crawled up in his lap and he would tell her stories about a princess and a bewildered prince. He called her his little princess, and in his make-believe stories, that was exactly who she became. She wasn't even sure what happened to her father. Kallie was convinced that her mother somehow drove him away. Anna had this way of pushing the people closest to her away. She was sure that it had to do with the fact Anna married and left home at seventeen. She was pregnant by eighteen, and Kallie assumed that it was just too much to handle at such a young age. Whenever Kallie asked about her father, her mother would say he just left them. Then she said she didn't want to discuss it anymore. When angry, Anna would suggest he probably managed to get himself arrested. Kallie wasn't sure why, but that never seemed right. She couldn't remember much, but she knew enough to know that her father was a good man. He seemed so kind and loving in the pictures. Nothing reasonable gave her the notion he would be in prison. Whatever the reason, it was obvious he didn't want to be with them or else he would have contacted them at one point or another.

Anna opened the closet door with a smile on her face.

"This is my favorite part. I miss playing dress up with my little girl."

"It is definitely good to see you smile, Mom," said Kallie with sincerity.

Anna's closet was huge. It was every teenage girl's dream. It was much more than a walk-in closet, it was a whole other room.

"Well baby girl, where are you going and what do you need?" Anna asked.

"I'm going to a get-together at Dane's house tomorrow night," answered Kallie.

"You mean a party," her mom said with a parent-like tone.

"Well, yeah. But it's not a big deal-"

"Kallie, I trust you! I trust you until you give me a reason not to. Lord knows I got into enough trouble as a kid for the both of us. You are a much better girl than I even thought about being."

Kallie was relieved. It had been only recently that she was formally invited onto the party scene. High school was a complete change from middle school. She'd always hung out with the "popular" kids, but now they were gaining opportunities for things they'd never done before. With Dane's parents going out of town and his older brother coming home from college, it was perfect timing. The football team didn't have a game Friday night, and their parents never expected James and Dane would have a party. Most parents assume their kids are more responsible than they actually are. Including college and high school kids, this party had the potential for setting records in the small town of Madison.

"Now tell me, Baby, how glamorous do you want to look for this party?" Anna asked with an intriguing grin.

Kallie smiled, "More glamorous than Shelby James would be great!"

"Aw, Baby, Shelby doesn't have anything on you. She *does*, however, tend to have herself all over every boy in this town. You are much better than her," Anna said.

"I just wanna stand out like she does. She shines where ever she goes. Every guy around will break his neck to get a look at her. I want a reaction like that. I don't want to be the only girl at school without a boyfriend."

"Rest assured, you are *NOT* the only girl at school without a boyfriend! Besides, maybe if you'd look a little closer, you'd notice that you *do* have admirers," Anna pressed her lips like she held a secret.

Anna remembered the day she saw little Ethan playing with his cars in the front yard. He was in second grade. Kallie swung from the tire tied to the tree in the front yard. It's almost funny, that particular moment in time when little boys change from thinking little girls are "yucky" to something more. Anna instinctively knew when she saw Ethan's effort to ignore Kallie that he was indeed very interested. And then, he built up the courage to walk across the yard to talk to her. Kallie was always very shy, especially as a child.

Ethan held out a car, "Would you like to come play cars with me? I'll let you have the silver one."

Kallie gave him a funny look and then replied with a simple "No."

Anna always hoped the two would become friends. But as fate would have it, Ethan was embarrassed and a long time passed before he spoke to Kallie again. Kallie spent the next couple of years trying to adapt to life without her father.

Anna's thoughts drifted back further to when she first met Kallie's father. Ray was amazing. He was everything she wanted and needed, and he was her hero. He rescued her from the life she so desperately needed to escape. She still loved him so much, and always hoped he would one day come back home.

Kallie, with a hint of curiosity in her voice, "Admirers, huh? And just how would *you* know?"

"Mothers know these things. Don't question it," Anna replied.

Kallie couldn't resist, "Well, you must have someone specific you are thinking about."

"There *is* a very handsome brown haired, brown eyed little boy that has watched you for quite some time now," Anna said.

"Mom!" exclaimed Kallie as she lowered the shirt she held, "Are you talking about Ethan again? He doesn't like me! He hardly ever talks to me. And when he does, it's as if he has to force himself to think of something to say."

Her mom laughed a little, "Give him a chance, maybe he's just a little shy?"

"I've tried talking to him, and I think he's slow or something. His social abilities are seriously lacking."

Kallie's phone made a buzzing sound. It was a text from Shelby.

"What are you doing?"

"I am standing in a closet with my mom."

"Uh, yeah ok. Closet?"

"Lol. She's letting me look at her clothes."

"That rocks! Your mom has totes awesome clothes!"

"I know, right!"

"kk, text me back when ur done."

"kk"

Anna pulled out a beautiful, emerald green top, "How about this one?"

Kallie was speechless and thought it was perfect.

"Green has always brought out the best in your eyes," Anna said as she smiled.

"It's perfect, Mom!" Kallie squealed.

"Well, try it on then!" Anna said as she handed it to Kallie.

It hugged Kallie's body in all the right places. This was surely going to get the reaction she wanted.

"And here, try it with *these* jeans," said Anna.

Kallie couldn't believe how impressive she looked. If only her mom dressed like this, maybe she'd get some attention also.

Kallie had to mention it, "Ya know mom, there's a new Algebra teacher that just transferred into this area. He's really cute too."

Knowing where Kallie intended to take the conversation, Anna quickly responded, "No Kallie! I've told you, I'm just fine by myself. You don't worry about me. You just take these on upstairs and worry about whatever boy you're trying to impress."

"If you insist," Kallie said taking the clothes from her mother. She wasn't going to argue. She had just been given the perfect outfit, and could hardly wait to tell Shelby. She carefully hung the clothes on her closet door and flopped on her bed.

Kallie texted Shelby:

"I can talk now. Guess what?"

"What?"

"My mom is letting me wear the most awesome green top!"

"Yay! I bet it's prettier than the one I have."

"I actually look really awesome in it, too!"

"We want you to look great, just as long as it's for the right people."

Kallie became aggravated, "And just who exactly are the right people?"

Shelby quickly answered, "I can tell you who it's NOT!"

Kallie answered back, "I just don't think it's fair for you to judge him like that. You don't know him."

"Come on, sister! He's way beneath you!" Shelby retorted.
"Maybe he's like my mom said, maybe he's just a little shy."

Kallie decoded the meanness in Shelby's text, "If his wings haven't bloomed by now, he's going to remain a social caterpillar. Face it!"

Kallie replied, "I just think there's something more to him."

It intrigued Kallie that Ethan lived next door to her all these years, yet she didn't know much about him. She sensed that there was something more to him than what everyone else could see.

"There are going to be college guys at this party. Just wait, you'll see," replied Shelby.

"All right Shelby. We'll see. Going to bed now. Goodnight."

"Nite nite."

Kallie lay awake in bed. She couldn't get comfortable with all the thoughts running through her mind. There was so much that she wanted to share with someone, but knew there wasn't really anyone she trusted. Shelby was all about the social scene and actually very superficial. Kallie and Shelby had been friends for years. Kallie never talked much about herself or things she went through. That was why she clicked so well with Shelby. Kallie never had to talk about herself because Shelby dominated every conversation with her own thoughts. Life seemed so confusing lately. As she closed her eyes and began to drift to sleep, she could see Ethan's face. Seeing him only confused her further. She felt drawn to him. She saw something different this year that she'd never seen before, and she wanted to know more.

Chapter 5

I couldn't believe it was already Friday. The entire week just flew by so quickly, and the strange things weren't any clearer. I had nightly dreams of strange people telling me they need me and warning me of an ever-present danger. The thing is, I finally came to the conclusion the dreams are, in some form, part of reality. They are definitely more than just dreams, or nightmares. I blocked out every class throughout the day today. I was only able to focus on finding some explanation for the strange people I'd been seeing, for the book and the way I found it, wondering what the book meant, and in between it all, still thinking about Kallie. My brain was certainly working overtime today.

As the final bell rang, everyone else had their minds on something other than school, also. The upcoming party tonight would be the talk of school for the next few weeks. The girls were giddy about what they were going to wear and the college guys they might see there. The guys were more concerned with the available alcohol and running their mouths about how much they'd consume.

Tucker sounded so hesitant, "Ethan man, are you sure you really want to go to this thing?"

"Yeah, why?" I asked.

"I don't know. Just that I'm not sure I feel like being a potential PUNCHING BAG for a bunch of drunken jocks," Tucker rolled his eyes as he spoke.

"Don't worry about it, Tuck. They'll be too wasted to even notice us there. I just think it's something we don't want to miss, ya know?"

Tucker smiled. "I think you just don't want to miss out on seeing a certain girl."

He was right, and I laughed a little, "Yeah well, that *is* part of it. I'd really like to try to talk to her tonight. I just don't know what to say. And I gotta catch her alone."

Tucker's eyes blinked rapidly as he wiped the sweat from his palms on his jeans. "Like I told you man, I'll go with you. But if it gets too rough, I'm leaving. I'd much rather get a good start on this project or something."

"That's fine, dude. Just give it a chance, that's all I ask. It may be just what we need to climb up that social ladder a little," I said with hope.

"I don't care about climbing. I've accepted the fact that I'm going to be the stool at the bottom and I'm fine with it," Tucker said.

Tucker's voice faded into mumbling, and I had this feeling that someone was watching us. Constantly looking over my shoulder, I felt it all the way home. Was I turning into some kind of paranoid freak or something? The warnings from my dream haunted me, yet, I felt so trapped not knowing how to respond. As

I arrived at home, I remembered my parents were working late. The house felt overly empty. Normally I would've asked Tucker to stay for a while, but I needed to sort some of these thoughts out. Earlier that day, I mentioned the book to Tucker and the strange writing in it. He suggested a few websites to begin my search in translating it. I didn't comment about seeing an illustration of the man from my dream. Being overly logical like he is, he would've come up with an intelligent explanation that would have made me think I was unreasonable with my emotions. Grasping how urgent the dreams were, I didn't want to be persuaded into minimizing whatever was going on.

The first thing I did was flip on the computer and got the book. I visited well over a hundred websites, and spent nearly three hours searching and still came up with nothing. There were similar writings, but nothing compared in the least. I had successfully caused myself further frustration.

I decided to give up for a while and began to get ready for the party. I usually take extremely long showers, and tonight wasn't an exception. I don't know what it is about the shower, but I can always clear my thoughts and come up with answers while showering. My eyes closed and the hot water rolled over my head and face. The water echoed as it hit the floor of the shower. It comforted me as it drained and washed away my unsettledness. The sound of the water got louder and my thoughts drifted into silence. I envisioned the man from my dreams. Afraid I was slipping back into a dream, my heart beat louder and louder.

Quickly, I opened my eyes to see an unusually thick fog filling the entire bathroom. The air possessed an unnatural and bizarre intensity. Then, someone, or something, touched the bathroom doorknob. I turned the water off and looked around for something to use as a weapon. Obviously, I was limited in options. I grabbed the closest object to me as if I was going to plunger someone to death, but it was the only thing I found. Wrapping the towel around my waist, I opened the door.

Tucker must have jumped a whole foot into the air as he squealed, "Crap! What the heck, man?"

"Sorry, Tucker, I thought I heard someone," I apologized.

"Paranoid much? You heard *me*. I told you I'd come over around eight. I knocked for like thirty minutes and then realized you left the door unlocked," explained Tucker.

"I guess I just lost track of time. Sorry, I didn't mean to scare you. You scared me first though," I told him.

I caught a glimpse of myself in the mirror. I stood there dripping wet with a plunger over my shoulder like a baseball bat. I had to laugh at myself, and Tucker contributed to the humorous sight by making jokes.

"And in the left corner, weighing in at 120 pounds, The Toilet Master," Tucker said between chuckles. "Now that's an image that would scare Dane into submission!"

"All right. Funny." I closed the bathroom door and dried off. I still heard Tucker in the bedroom getting a good laugh out of it. I rummaged through my closet and got dressed. Tucker was sitting at my desk when I came out.

"Ethan, this book is really old, dude. This is cool. I wonder if it is some form of fiction or something. Did you look at these images?" Tucker asked with amazement.

"Yeah, I did. I think maybe they were real people or something."

"I doubt it. Look at these. They had a light, or wind, or something coming from their hands. It's like they had powers or something. We'll look into translating this a little later. I'm sure we can find someone who can help," Tucker was quite confident.

"So how do I look?" I asked.

Tucker laughed, "Like Ethan. You look like yourself."

My nerves surged out of control. I really needed to make a good impression on Kallie. I just wanted the opportunity to talk to her for a few minutes.

"I'm serious. Do I look all right?" I asked again.

"You look fine, Man. Don't stress," Tucker replied.

"I just want her to notice me," I said.

"I just want to go absolutely *unnoticed*," Tucker said with uncertainty.

I felt completely different though.

"It'll be great. I have this feeling that tonight is going to be amazing."

One last look in the mirror, a spray of cologne, and we were gone. It was a little after nine, yet the moon was so bright we didn't need the streetlights to see. The music got louder as we neared Dane's house. There were cars lined down both sides of the street and in the yard. It looked like a carnival or something. Other than the music being loud, it was still fairly calm. The front door and side gates were open, and people were freely coming and going. We went in the side gate that led to the pool and hot tub. There must have been thirty or more college girls in their swimsuits. Tucker and I looked at each other with amazement, and he produced a funny grin on his face.

"Oh yeah, this was a good idea," he said standing there in awe.

Dane and Rodney were inside with others gathered around the TV. They were reviewing their great plays from last week's game. James was at the outside bar mixing drinks for the crowd. There was a small group of high school girls beginning to gather around him. We grabbed a bottle of water and decided to sit out of the way. I agreed with Tucker and didn't mind just sitting and watching the view for a while.

We'd been there for quite some time when a loud scream came from inside the house. It was Shelby James. Dane let out a large growl and scooped her up and headed toward the pool. Shelby was kicking, screaming, and begging. He acted as though he was going to throw her in, but the look on his face showed he was just flirting with her. Flirting quickly turned into a public show of making out.

As everyone began to lose interest in watching Shelby and Dane, I saw the one thing I was there for. Kallie and Megan walked out the back door. The patio lights reflected off Kallie's hair and she looked more spectacular than ever before. Everything else around me ceased to exist. I didn't even bother to say anything to Tucker and just headed straight to her. I was overly confident, and knew this was my one shot. She would either talk to me or I needed to give up for good.

I tapped her on the shoulder and caught a glimpse of her scent as she turned around.

"Oh. Hi, Ethan. I wasn't sure if you'd be here or not." She had sincere delight in her voice.

"I wasn't going to miss the biggest party in Madison history," I said.

She laughed, "Me either. It'll definitely be the talk of the town for a while."

"You look really great tonight," The words left my mouth faster than they processed through my brain.

She was blushing, "Thanks. It's the shirt. It-"

I interrupted her. "It's not the shirt. It's you. You always look great."

There was no doubt I embarrassed her. "Thanks, Ethan. That's really- sweet," she said.

Megan turned toward us, "Kallie, I'm going to go hang out by the bar for a little while. Take your time and come find me when you get done talking to Ethan."

Megan winked at Kallie as she walked away. She was always a little more accepting of me than Shelby.

"I'm sorry. I didn't mean to take you away from your friend," I apologized.

"No. It's okay. I'd rather stay and talk for a little while." Her eyes sparkled as she spoke.

There was an old tire swing hanging from a tree toward the back part of the yard.

I pointed it out and said, "How about we go over there so I can hear you a little more clearly?"

"Sounds great," she agreed.

She always looked so graceful in everything she did. From walking across the yard, to climbing into the tire, I couldn't take my eyes off her.

"Push me?" she suggested.

I couldn't think of what to say as she gently swayed back and forth. Time passed by so quickly. I got caught up in watching her hair blow in the breeze. Her scent captivated me, yet the look in her eyes showed her discontentment.

I broke the silence, "Kind of strange, isn't it?"

"What's that?" she asked with curiosity.

"That we've lived next door to each other since we were little, yet we have only actually talked a handful of times," I answered.

She responded honestly, "Yeah, I suppose it is strange. I guess I've just always kind of kept to myself."

"Why is that?" I asked.

Her voice softened, "I don't know. Maybe something I've learned from my mom. I guess I'm just really cautious about letting people into my life."

"Not exactly healthy, you know," I responded.

"I know," she said.

Not wanting her to think I was judging her, I replied, "Don't get me wrong, I understand. I've had a lot of things, especially here lately, that I can't talk to anyone about either."

Kallie got a distant look in her eyes, "At least you have your family. Family is supposed to always be there for you."

"I take it that your mom isn't very understanding?" I asked.

"It's not so much that she doesn't understand as it is that she's filled up with her own problems and depression," she replied.

"Oh really? I've talked to her a few times when she's been outside and she seems normal," I said.

She nodded a little, "I guess you'd just have to know her better. She puts on a good show, but she's really lonely."

The swing slowed and her eyes met mine. I was whispering at this point. "It's not good for people to be lonely."

"No, it's not," she said as she smiled.

"Everyone needs someone they can share secrets with," I said as I moved a little closer.

"Then it wouldn't be considered a secret anymore," she seemed distracted as she spoke.

"It'd be nice to have someone to share all your thoughts and dreams with. Even the nightmares," I spoke slowly as she began to put her arms around me.

I wished I could tell her about some of the things I'd heard and seen lately. I knew it would scare her and she'd think I was crazy.

Tucker's voice interrupted, "Ethan! I've been looking everywhere for you."

"Uh, yeah Tucker. We kind of came over here to be alone."

"Oh. Sorry. Well, I'm not sure if you noticed or not, but the natives are getting kind of crazy." Tucker looked around anxiously. "I think I'm going to head home."

The sound of glass shattering came from the house. Dane was yelling about something but we couldn't understand him. James was trying to calm him down. James' voice was loud and firm, "I said go somewhere and calm down NOW!"

Dane took his drink and slung it into the pool. He disappeared with Rodney and two others through the gate and into the front. The sound of squealing tires filled the air as they drove away.

"Yeah, I see what you mean, Tuck," I agreed.

"I told you I'd come to this thing with you, but I'm not going to get busted over it. It won't be long before more trouble finds its way here," Tucker said.

"All right man. Give me just another minute and we'll go." I motioned to help Kallie out of the tire.

"You don't have to leave. I'm a big boy and can find my way home," Tucker nodded his head toward Kallie understanding the importance of the situation.

Kallie spoke up, "Actually, it's about time for me to head home as well."

I was relieved, "If Kallie is ready to go, we'll catch right up to you, Tuck. I was going to offer to walk her home anyway, so we'll be right there."

Tucker quickly said, "I'm out of here, guys. Take your time. I'll call you tomorrow, Ethan."

Kallie grabbed my shoulders and I helped her out of the swing. She was very clumsy and nearly fell. I could tell it was just an act, especially since she always had terrific balance. I helped her up anyway.

She said, "Thanks. Guess it's been a while since I've climbed out of one of those."

"No problem," I said enjoying every second.

"Let me go tell Shelby and Megan I'm leaving," she said.

"Okay. I'll wait over by the gate for you," I assured her.

Kallie disappeared into the house. I couldn't believe that she was actually talking to me. She even flirted with me. I felt so awesome. It was hard to act cool and not show my heart was actually about to pound out of my chest.

Kallie saw Megan and Shelby sitting on the stairs, Shelby crying. Kallie remembered Dane's angry outburst and hurried over to the girls.

"Oh, what happened, Shelby?" Kallie asked.

Shelby sobbed and held her hands over her face.

Megan answered for her, "Dane and Shelby got into an argument. He thought some guy flirted with her and went off."

In between breaths, Shelby said, "I told Dane that he was just talking to me, but he wouldn't listen. It wasn't a big deal. Honest it wasn't."

Kallie tried to comfort her, "It wasn't your fault, Sweetie. Dane is like that. He'll go find something to take it out on and everything will be back to normal."

"I'm about to take her home," said Megan.

"I'm headed home, too," said Kallie.

Megan pulling out her keys said, "Ok, let's load up then."

"Actually, I'm going to walk home," Kallie said with a smile.

"Not alone you aren't," Megan raised her voice with concern.

"Ethan is going to walk me," Kallie clarified.

Megan smiled, but Shelby began to cry even harder.

Shelby sobbed something about Ethan when Megan interrupted her, "Shel, you've had too much to drink and it's time to get some rest. You can sleep it off at my house tonight."

Megan and Kallie helped Shelby stand up. Kallie watched as they made their way out the door toward Megan's car.

I began to wonder if everything was all right when I heard Kallie's voice, "Sorry that took so long. I'm ready now."

"Everything okay?" I asked.

"Yeah, evidently Dane and Shelby got into it. She'll be fine after he cools down and the alcohol wears off."

We walked home slowly, and I was completely caught up in our conversation. We discussed a lot of things. Mostly things from when we were younger.

"So what is the strangest or scariest thing that's ever happened to you?" Kallie asked.

I instantly wanted to tell her it has been the last few days, but I knew I couldn't. I would love to be able to tell someone about my dreams and the things I've seen and know they believed me and understood. I knew it wasn't the time though. This was something I'd have to figure out on my own. I thought it best to tell her about the time I fell out of a tree. Kind of silly, but it answered the question.

"So how about you? Strangest or scariest thing," I asked.

A distressed look appeared on Kallie's face.

"I haven't really talked about it in a long time, but I suppose since I brought it up, it's only fair that I have to answer in return," she said.

I wanted to know, but I didn't want her to discuss something upsetting to her.

"It's okay if you don't want to talk about it," I said.

"I'm okay." She struggled with the words. "I guess I'd have to say the time that my dad left us. I had a really hard time with it. My mom tried, but she didn't know how to help me deal with it. I panicked one night and all I can remember is crying and running away to go look for him. I got lost, and it was pretty scary."

"I remember that," I replied.

I remembered hearing my parents discuss how horrible it was that little Kallie had gone missing. The police were next door for several days in a row. The whole town was on a mad hunt trying to find her.

"There were a lot of rumors about that for a while," I mentioned. "You know, things like your dad had come back into town and kidnapped you."

"I wish. I mean… I know that sounds strange, just that I wish it had been that simple. I've really missed my dad over the years. I don't think he's ever wanted anything to do with us though. It's messed with me not having him around," she said.

"So, you just ran away?" I asked.

"I guess. Honestly, I'd rather talk about something else now."

"Sure. Next question?"

I wondered what the rest of the story was. I remembered the whole town fearing a kidnapper was in the area. And then like nothing ever happened, she just showed up back at home one day. Rumors were still around for years after, but no one ever knew what really happened. Most people believed that Anna was so upset over Ray leaving that she staged the whole thing in hopes it would bring him home. Needless to say, Anna was always looked at differently after that week.

We were home. It occurred to me that Tucker wasn't around. I had gotten so caught up in our conversation that we must have walked a little slower than I intended.

"I guess Tuck probably went on to his house," I suggested.

"We *have* been walking for a while," she replied.

I couldn't believe it had been that long.

"You think? It doesn't seem like much time passed by," I said.

Kallie laughed a little, "We just turned a fifteen minute walk into an hour and a half."

I was amazed the time with her passed so quickly. She was amazing. Consumed with everything she said throughout the night, I was more excited than ever that we were talking. As I was going to tell her how much I enjoyed spending time with her, she once again caught me off guard and leaned in towards me. Her lips were soft as they pressed against my cheek. Two inches to the left and they would've been touching mine. I was speechless.

"Thanks for walking me home, Ethan," she said.

"Uh, no problem," I uttered.

"I really enjoyed talking to you tonight," she whispered.

"I really enjoyed you talking to me tonight also." I realized how stupid I probably sounded. "Have a good night, Kallie."

I stood motionless as she disappeared into her house. Everything else in life ceased to exist and all my thoughts were consumed with Kallie. As I lay down in bed for the night, I relived every moment of the night, especially the kiss. Had I known it was going to happen, maybe I could've responded differently. I drifted off to sleep with thoughts of what destiny held in store for me.

Chapter 6

I woke up to the sound of a loud slamming door and yelling voices. Still dazed from sleep, I tried to determine if I was dreaming. I became fully awakened when I realized it was Tucker's parents I heard. It wasn't unusual to have strange awakenings for me, but it was very unusual to hear Tucker's parents on a Saturday morning. I could only imagine the trouble he must have gotten into for being caught at Dane's party. Wondering how I could make it up to him for going against his better judgment, I got dressed and headed downstairs. Judy, Tucker's mom, sat at the kitchen table with her hands shaking as she wiped the tears from her face. I looked around for Tucker, but he wasn't there. Instantly, all eyes turned towards me as if they were anticipating a certain reaction.

"What's going on?" I asked without a clue.

My mom expressed deep concern, "Tucker never made it home last night. Judy and Alan stayed up all night waiting for him and he never showed. They came over here first thing this morning hoping to find him."

I didn't fully understand. I was still groggy and shook my head in disbelief.

"We thought maybe he stayed the night here, but I checked your room this morning and he wasn't in there," she continued.

I was shocked and completely confused by what I heard. "That's not like him to do something like that," I said.

"We know, Ethan." My dad gave me a sort of irritated glance as he tilted his head toward Tucker's concerned parents. "We were hoping you'd have a helpful suggestion as to where he might be. Judy and Alan spoke with the police this morning, but they said until he's missing for at least twenty-four hours, they won't begin looking for him."

"It just doesn't make any sense. He seemed fine last night when he said he was going home," I mumbled to myself.

"What time did he leave here, Ethan?" Mom asked.

Realizing that our parents still didn't know we were at Dane's house, I wasn't sure how to respond.

"He said you guys were going to be working on some project for school," Tucker's dad said, as tears formed in the corner of his eyes.

I couldn't lie. Something was wrong, and as much trouble as we'd both get in for being there, it just wasn't like Tucker to go off without telling someone.

"I suppose it was around eleven or a little after when he left," I said. No point in giving more details than necessary, I thought to myself.

My mom turned to Judy, and said, "Mike and I didn't get home last night until after midnight. Ethan was already asleep, so he had to of been gone sometime before then."

There had to be a reasonable explanation for this. Without saying anything further, I ran upstairs and got my backpack and put my shoes on.

"Where are you going?" Mom asked.

"I'm going to find Tucker! Maybe he's at the library or something." My thoughts were scattered. "We were supposed to be working on this project this weekend, maybe that's exactly what he's doing," I answered.

"Ethan, the library isn't open that late on a Friday night," Alan said with frustration.

"I know that, sir. But there has to be an explanation and sitting around here isn't going to help find him," I replied as I ran out of the house.

I headed to the library. I knew fully well Tucker wasn't there, but I wasn't sure where else to go. I replayed the night over in my mind trying to remember something he may have said, but nothing stood out. The library was at the end of the street past Dane's house and the school. I looked closely at Dane's house as I walked by. Other than some trash on the front lawn, everything looked quiet and normal. My pace began to turn into a light jog as I became more concerned.   Suddenly, a flash of light caused me to go completely blind. I tripped and fell to the ground. Lying there for just a moment, I caught my breath. As I gained my sight back, I looked around to see what caused it. The wind started to blow fiercely, and I was able to see the school building. The wind pushed me towards the school as I stood back up. A familiar drumming sound filled the background noise. It was the same sound I heard so many times before in my dreams. A small twinkle of light shone through the main doors of the school. Instinct told me I needed to pursue it. The wind was so strong and it became even stronger as I neared the front of the school. My feet were actually being lifted off the ground. Then as quick as it had begun, the wind stopped as my hand touched the door. I heard nothing, not a bird chirp, not a kid playing in the neighborhood, not even a car passing by. It was if time was standing still. The door slammed behind me as I entered. I realized how ridiculous it was to be in the school, and how much trouble I'd get in for being there after school hours. The more I thought about it, I wondered *why* the doors were unlocked to begin with.

I turned to leave, and noticed something on the floor; shoe skid marks. Being in high school, it was typical to see skid marks, but these were different. They were solid, not like intentional footsteps. I followed them down the hall and around the first set of lockers. Occasionally, they broke up as if the feet were lifted and then dragged some more. Then they stopped all together. Papers and books were all over the place. Then it occurred to me, this wasn't just *any* locker. It belonged to Tucker. I felt sick to my stomach not being able to understand what I saw. Tucker's locker caved inward. I tried to open it, but it was almost impossible because the wedge caused by the dents. It finally came loose when I thought my strength had given out. I fell to my knees when I saw what was inside. It was completely empty except for Tucker's glasses. I didn't have any doubt they were his. Where was Tucker though? I held his glasses in my hand as if they were going to somehow answer me and tell me what happened. Then, I heard a noise. I wasn't alone in the school.

"What are you doing here, boy?"

The voice startled me. A janitor was standing in the hallway behind me. He was very tall and wore some kind of safety glasses covered in paint. I figured he was probably there painting over the weekly slander written on the bathroom walls.

"Did you hear me? I said what are you doing here?" he said again.

He spoke with a frightening tone the second time. I tried to think of something that wouldn't get me into further trouble when he started walking towards me.

"I was uh…. Um…," I stuttered.

As the words tried to form a complete sentence, something caught my eye, a bright golden object hanging from a belt loop on his overalls. It was the same one I had seen on the man in the library. Suddenly, just as if I was in a dream, I heard a voice loud and clear, "RUN, EITAN!"

I scrambled to my feet and began to run around the corner toward the front door. The man stopped walking, but I still felt him breathing down my neck. As the front doors came into view, something black and scaly covered them blocking my exit. I quickly turned to find another way out. The black scales covered all of the windows and classroom doors.

"You have something that doesn't belong to you, Eitan!" he demanded.

"Tucker's glasses? Why would you want Tucker's glasses?" I asked.

"Glasses are NOT what we are interested in!" he shouted.

The man placed his long fingers around his own glasses and removed them. I knew him. His eyes were that same empty gray color I had seen twice before. A cold chill filled my body I froze. I panicked as he walked toward me. Like so many times before, I heard my own heart about to beat out of my chest. I was trapped. Intense power radiated from him. Unaware of what was going on, my own hands were getting hot like they were on fire. I looked down to see large sparks and light emitting from them. The man stopped coming towards me. The look on his face changed from anger to concern. My legs walked backwards toward the doors. I closed my eyes and within an instant, felt great power come from my hands. It was as though they exploded. I was surrounded by light, and with the next step backward, I was falling. The man yelling in anger, but all I could see was blackness and flashes of bright green light. The wind crackled louder than I ever heard it before. It was like I had been swept up in a tornado. Without warning, my whole body hit something hard, the ground. I wanted to open my eyes but I couldn't. I couldn't move. My thoughts drifted from what I hoped was just a bad dream, to knowing it wasn't.

Chapter 7

Tucker felt terrible about interrupting Ethan while he finally got conversation time with Kallie. He didn't intend for Ethan to leave and accompany him home, but he also didn't feel right just leaving and not letting him know. Although, as wrapped up in Kallie Thompson as he was, Ethan probably wouldn't have even noticed. Tucker glanced back as he reached the side gate and noticed as Kallie fell clumsily into Ethan's arms. Tucker laughed to himself realizing how much Ethan probably enjoyed the attention she was giving him. Tucker decided to go ahead and start walking home. After all, he didn't want to be the third wheel all the way home, and it would give Ethan some much deserved time with Kallie.

Tucker thought about the research he'd found, and how he was going to bring together all the details into a captivating presentation that would deliver him yet another "A". As he turned the corner, squealing tires interrupted his thoughts. The sound of a growling engine was not far behind him. His shadow grew to twenty feet tall as the headlights beamed on his backside. The one situation he avoided all night was front and center. He barely heard what was being said over the revving of the engine, but he knew who it was. He turned around just as the shrieking noise of spinning tires moved toward him. He quickly jumped out of the way and remained on the ground as the car sped by him. He hoped the car would continue on down the road, but hopes faded when he heard it stop. As the car turned around, Tucker swiftly jumped to his feet and ran. There wasn't any possible way to outrun the car, but he ran through yards and over fences to escape. Surely Dane and his friends wouldn't destroy the neighborhood by running the car through yards. After jumping the third fence, he slowed down. He didn't hear the car anymore. Exhausted, he took his last bit of energy and made his way back toward the sidewalk. Dane's car sat parked on the curb about three houses away and the headlights were off. Everything was fairly quiet except for the distant noise coming from the party at Dane's house. Tucker placed his hands on his knees in relief as he caught his breath.

Unexpectedly, a voice shouted from the darkness, "I found the jerk! Over here!"

It was Rodney. He couldn't see which direction Rodney was coming from, but by judging where the voice was, Tucker turned to the right and began running again. He just needed one good place to hide until they got bored with the cat and mouse game and then he'd safely sneak home. The schoolyard gate was open, and he made a dash for his hideaway. The auto shop would have someplace decent to lie low. A strong punch to his chest cut his mad dash short. The blow sent him collapsing to the ground. He couldn't think straight. All thoughts were jumbled and focused on one specific thing- the amount of pain protruding from his chest. Rodney's voice was clear as he felt himself lifted off the ground. His feet were dragged along the sidewalk. As the haze lifted from his eyes, he saw Dane walking in front of them. They headed toward the school. Nick Collinger's voice expressed concern as he murmured to Dane. Nick was always the weakest of their pack.

"Nick! Shut up! If you're concerned, go home!" Dane said with irritation in his voice.

"It's just that we have a big game coming up, and Coach says if we get into any more trouble, we can't play," Nick said.

Nick's pleas began to sink in.

"Listen. We aren't going to do anything to get us in trouble. We're just gonna rough him up a bit," Dane said.

Tucker, becoming more aware of what was going on, put up resistance as they neared the front of the school.

"You know you can't just go in there!" Tucker said weakly in between breaths. Dane took a key from his pocket and unlocked the front door as if it were his own house.

"How's that work out for you, Nerd?" Dane said as he punched Tucker in the stomach.

They were headed into the school, and he envisioned all the torment he was about to endure. He put up a tremendous fight but it wasn't helping. Their grip was too tight on him. Their laughter and excitement did nothing more than multiply his fear. Dane kicked and punched the lockers as they dragged him down the halls. Tucker gave up the struggle and he was released. Dane pried open Tucker's locker.

"Get in, or we *put* you in!" Dane ordered.

Tucker remained motionless on the floor. He was much smaller than most of the football players. In fact, he was even smaller than the water boys. Nevertheless, he wasn't sure he would fit inside the locker even if he wanted to.

"Are you stupid? Did you not hear him? Get in!" Rodney confirmed the order.

Tucker lifted himself off the ground and his head tilt side to side weighing the choices. He was shoved hard. Within seconds, his entire body crumpled into a position even a human contortionist would find uncomfortable. The locker door slammed and an explosion of laughter came from the hallway. Tucker begged and screamed for help, hoping that somehow someone would hear him. He pushed his feet against the door expecting it to cave in to the pressure, but it didn't. The voices became more distant, which made him panic all the more. Without warning, Tucker saw a bright flash of light and felt himself being sucked and pulled through a vacuum. His body released itself from the uncomfortable position. The force of the wind was very strong, yet it was as if someone held him up. He thought maybe Rodney felt sorry for him and released him.

Dane laughed as he replayed the scene in his mind. He got sick joy from listening to Tucker beg for help. The fact Tucker became increasingly louder added to Dane's amusement. Dane turned to take one last look at the rattling locker when he was paralyzed by an intense burst of light that came from it. Tucker was quiet and no longer screaming for help. Dane's vision cleared, and he noticed the struggle going on inside the locker stopped. He was tempted to walk toward it in order to further investigate the situation when Rodney slammed through the front door.

"Come on, Dane! Someone is coming!" Rodney said with urgency.

"Look," Dane said. He pointed to the locker, "He isn't screaming or moving," Dane said in a slow and confused voice.

"Dane, he's just trying to trick you so you'll open it. Come on man, or we are going to get busted!"

Vividly aware of the consequences if caught, Dane quickly followed Rodney down the sidewalk and back to the car. All the while, he was still overly concerned about what he just witnessed.

Tucker couldn't decide. Was he dead or dreaming? Maybe he was having a complete out of body experience. He was definitely glad his body was out of that position. Consciously aware he now stood in an upright position, he reached to adjust his glasses. The fact they were not on his face explained why his vision remained blurred. He attempted to focus on his surroundings in order to better grasp where he was.

"It's not him!" said a voice to his left.

Another voice spoke from his right, "It has to be. We've all had a part in this. Are you suggesting we were wrong?"

"I'm suggesting that it's not *him*, take it how you want," replied the first voice.

Large hands grabbed his shoulders from behind. The voice belonging to those hands spoke, "It is pointless to discuss it. Take your hand and see if the veranum is revealed. If we have failed, let the blame be on us *all*."

Tucker's chest tightened. All the voices were unrecognizable. His sight became clearer, along with the fact he was no longer at the school. He dared to speak, but desperately needed clarification.

"Who are you people? Where am I?" Tucker asked as his head got pushed down. A cold hand pressed on the back of his neck.

"Where am I?" Tucker asked again.

The voices were more panicked in tone.

"It's not there!"

"Bloody hell, Marik!" shouted a new voice, "Are you sure it isn't there?"

"I'm not blind! Yes, I'm sure!"

Tucker struggled while being held.

He repeated, "I said, where am I? Who are you people? What do you want with me?"

Still being ignored, the voices continued, "Well, what do you propose we do now, Sir Marik?"

The voice spoke with condescension and sarcasm.

The man behind him took an authoritative tone.

"Enough! We have bigger problems on our hands now! We *must* find him before Kiverus does!"

"Maybe we haven't completely failed. Is this guy a Candraen? Maybe he can help? After all, Kiverus was searching there, which if nothing else, means we were in the right place. That's at least something."

Tucker's head was released and he saw several people standing very close to him. Their faces displayed deep concern and frustration. A tall slender man stood to his left.

The man had a deep, stern tone when he spoke, "Hold out your left hand."

Instinct told him he'd better do as asked. The small crowd huddled closer to him, and he lifted his arm to reveal his palm.

"He's not a Candraen either. He doesn't even know what you are looking for," whispered a frustrated voice from the crowd.

"Turn your hand over," requested the tall man.

Tucker stood motionless. He didn't have whatever it was they were looking for, but was concerned what they were going to do with him.

He attempted to ask one more time, "Who are you? Why have you brought me here?"

The man grabbed Tucker's hand and flipped it over. He then placed his own left hand under Tucker's. Everyone's eyes were fixed on the hands. After a few seconds passed, the man lowered his hand and released Tucker's. The crowd sighed in defeat.

"I told you," said a short burly man with lots of hair.

He gave Tucker a scowling glare and walked away. The others began to disperse from the crowd also. They gathered around a small table in the corner as their faces and demeanor were consumed with disappointment.

A younger man moved closer to Tucker and spoke in a quiet voice. "What now, Samuil?"

The tall slender man replied, "I don't know Marik. I just know we can't give up. Our fate is determined by our actions."

Samuil turned and walked until he disappeared into a dark hallway. For the first time since his arrival, Tucker examined his surroundings. Things were slightly blurry without his glasses, but he saw enough to tell he was in some sort of a cave. There weren't any windows and the air contained an old rustic smell. The sound of running water was in the distance. The men sat around the table conversing in quiet voices. Occasionally, they looked over at Tucker as if he had some sort of disease or infection.

It startled Tucker when the young man placed his hand on his shoulder and spoke to him. "I'm sorry to drag you into this friend. We sort of confused you with someone else."

"What am I doing here? I don't understand," Tucker replied.

"There's a lot that you don't understand, and probably aren't going to understand," said Marik.

"How did I get here? Last thing I remember, I was crammed and stuck inside my school locker."

Marik chuckled slightly, "Is that what that was? Don't guess I'd complain about being here if I were you then. This should definitely be more comfortable."

"Aren't you going to take me home now?" Tucker asked.

Marik turned serious, "You can't go home right now. I don't know what they will decide to do with you."

"*Do* with me?" Tucker asked with confusion. "No one asked me if I wanted to come here. I don't want to be here. I want to go home."

"Do you want me to take you back to your locker? Seriously?" Stress apparent on Marik's face, "Listen, it's fine," Marik continued, "We aren't going to harm you. I just don't know how to approach this. If we take you back now, we risk getting caught by Kiverus. We can't take that kind of a chance. Not now." Marik's face was consumed with deep thoughts.

"I don't mean to be rude, but I don't know who Kiverus is. I certainly don't know where I am, nor do I know any of you people. There will be family and friends at home looking for me if I don't go back," Tucker tried to sound persuasive.

"Your people are the last thing we are concerned with at the moment," said Marik.

Tucker sighed with frustration. It concerned him. Once again he was in a hopeless situation that appeared it wasn't going to end well.

Marik spoke apologetically, "I'm sorry. I know this must be confusing and frustrating for you. Where you are from, it is getting late. You should be tired by now. Come with me and I'll show you somewhere you can rest until we figure something out."

Marik motioned his hand down a dimly lit hallway.

"Follow me, there are rooms and beds down this way," Marik said.

The lack of light made it even harder for Tucker to see. Marik opened a door and walked inside.

"You expect me to sleep?" Tucker asked.

"I expect you to rest. You aren't going to be treated as a prisoner, but please understand that you cannot leave. If you get hungry, we have plenty of food here. Once you've rested, you can come back to the main room and find me. We will talk, and I will try to answer some of your questions," Marik offered.

Tucker reluctantly sat on the edge of the bed, and Marik left the room. How could he possibly rest after everything that happened that night? He tried to reason what happened. Nothing came to mind. He *was* exhausted. He decided to lie down and get a little more comfortable since it looked like he was going to have an extended stay. He watched the doorway and the different people that passed by. It caught him off guard when a woman carrying a baby walked by. It didn't seem like the kind of place for children. There was a smaller child, probably three or four years old holding onto the woman's skirt. The child paused briefly at the door to get a look at the new visitor. She raised her hand and waived at him. Tucker gave her a slight smile before she giggled and ran off. He took a deep breath and closed his eyes, only for just a minute.

Chapter 8

Tucker opened his eyes and reached toward the nightstand for his glasses. They weren't there. Realization came surging back. He glanced at the clock hanging on the wall. It relieved him to know he hadn't fallen asleep considering it showed the same time as when he closed his eyes.

Some laughter came from the other room and he decided it was time to find out what was going on. As he entered the main room, he was greeted by a group of men with very serious faces. The laughter must have come from the small group of ladies sitting at the table.

A younger girl appeared in the shadows of one of the many hallways. She walked over to Tucker with a welcoming smile on her face. Her voice was gentle when she spoke.

"Are you hungry?" she asked.

As if it were a trick question, he answered cautiously, "A little?"

Tucker was hungry, but still had reservations about these strangers. He wasn't sure if it was safe to eat with them or not.

"Follow me. I'll show you where the dining area is," she said as she motioned.

It was strange how dark the hallways were until walking down them and light just appeared to guide them. She led him to a table and told him to make himself at home. He'd give just about anything if he *were* at home right now. He sat down at the table and noticed the unusual fruit sitting in a bowl at the center of the table. The fruit was the most unique color of purple. It sparkled and resembled a large kiwi. She took a fruit and offered it to him. He barely touched the outside with his tongue and the taste was amazing. It tasted as if it was covered in sugar, and the sweetness continued into the fleshy center.

"What is your name?" Tucker tried to ask in between bites.

"Abigeal. What is your name?" she asked in return.

"My name is Tucker."

"Tucker," she said with a smile, "that is an unusual name."

Abigeal poured something that looked like tea into a small sipping cup. Her eyes never left his as she sprinkled green leaves into it. She nodded her head for Tucker to take it and drink. Tucker hesitated, but considering the fruit was so delicious, he couldn't resist. The steam rising from it revealed it was extremely hot. He pressed his lips and took a small sip.

"It's not the best tasting stuff, but I think you'll like the effect it has," she said.

Tucker noticed instantly his eyesight was clearer. He turned to Abigeal only to notice her satisfied smile.

"What is this stuff? That's amazing," he said to her.

"There is a river that runs close to here. Special fruit trees line both sides of the river. The fruit provides abounding energy while the leaves provide healing. I expect you will need both."

She handed him a small bag that contained more fruit and a bottle of the tea. The tea was surely drugged because he noticed her beauty more and more. He tried to shake the feeling, but it wasn't the tea, or the fruit. It was that his eyes finally focused where they should, and she was purely magnificent. She was reserved and elegant despite her young age. She certainly would have put shame to any girl in Madison. Her hair was so dark it appeared like black silk as it flowed exquisitely around her waist, and her eyes reminded him of blue morning glories in his grandmother's garden.

He hoped she would be able to clarify some of the questions running through his mind.

"Abigeal," intrigued by just the sound of her name, "do you know why I was brought here?"

A voice answered from behind him, "We all know why you were brought here. But *we* have many questions that need answered as well."

"Good evening, Marik," she said.

Abigeal had been caught off guard.

"Hello, Abigeal. You look nice tonight. It's my regret that time will not allow me to stay and chat, but our visitor has been requested to come meet with the high council," Marik replied.

It sounded serious to Tucker. "High council? Who are they? Why?"

Marik laughed, "Friend, you have a lot of questions. Follow me and we'll get some answers for you. Bring your food if you like."

Tucker arose from the table and followed Marik. He looked back and saw Abigeal cleaning his place. He wished he could stay longer.

"Thank you for the food. It was delicious," he called back to her while following Marik.

Her smile grew and he noticed what a beautiful smile she had.

"I'm sure we will see each other again, Tucker." She turned and disappeared back down another hallway.

Amazing. His eyesight already altered enough it was if he was wearing his glasses. He examined Marik while following him. Marik was in his early twenties. His physical appearance was robust and powerful. He had a rugged hairstyle, yet his face appeared gentle. Everyone seemed to have similar wardrobe resembling a monk's attire. They entered a darkened room lit by a fire and several candles. The high council consisted of five men. The introduction wasn't too alarming with the exception of one man who made Tucker extremely uncomfortable. He was much older than the rest, and he didn't speak. He looked like an old Indian chief with long, white, and braided hair. He had so many wrinkles his eyes were hard to see, yet Tucker felt them inspecting his every move.

"My name is Samuil," spoke the tall slender man from earlier. He pointed from his left to right, "This is Lucan, Aeacus, and Jacen."

Lucan was very pale in color. He was bald on his head, but had a greyish goatee that made him seem distinguished. Aeacus was shorter than the others and a bit overweight. His blond hair partly covered his left eye and made it difficult for Tucker to interpret the man's thoughts. Jacen was, by far, the tallest and largest. His hair was cut short, and there was no doubt that he was the strongest. Jacen played with a dagger he held in his hands making the situation more intense.

Samuil's face became reverent as he introduced the older man, "This is Caedmius. He is our wisest and eldest family member."

The men all nodded and acknowledged Tucker except Caedmius who was motionless. He just stared intently at Tucker.

"Please, sit down," Samuil said, resuming his own seat, "We have taken you from your home and without your permission. For that, I am sorry. Please try to understand there is a much larger problem at hand. There are forces at work and people with tremendous power they should not possess. You were taken because of incorrect assumptions that led us to believe you were the one that would save our people."

Tucker spoke hesitantly, "Forgive me for asking, but who *are* your people? And save your people from what?"

Samuil replied, "We are called Candraens. Candraens are being captured, and some murdered under the orders of the one named Kiverus. There is so much that people from your world don't understand. It makes it hard for me to explain."

Tucker further confused, "*My* world? If we aren't in *my* world, where are we? How many *worlds* are there?"

Samuil answered, "The thing most frustrating about people from your world is that, generation after generation, they continue to inhibit their thoughts in a way that leads them to believe theirs is the only world in existence. It's very selfish and egotistical actually. I will try to explain this in a way your mind will allow you to understand."

Tucker understood one thing, the condescending tone that was used toward him.

Samuil continued, "Kiverus is a Lathiaen. The Lathiaens were a group of people chosen and deemed worthy of maintaining the balance and order among the different worlds. Among several other powers, the Lathiaens were given the ability to travel back and forth to the different worlds in order to perform their duties. Many centuries ago, there was a Lathiaen who had fallen in love with a mortal. It was against the Lathiaen law for them to be together. Yet, despite the law, they continued their relationship and eventually had a child together. This child became the first Candraen. He learned early in life he was able to travel between the different worlds also. However, he did not inherit all of the other powers. Through the years, the Candraen people continued to grow in population, and continued to pass along the ability to travel. There have always been groups of Lathiaens that remain enraged and angered by the fact that Candraens exist. The Lathiaens, as a whole, are very righteous and honorable people. The problem remains with the few who are not. Kiverus has gained undeserved control of the Lathiaen people and has enlisted several followers whom have vowed to destroy all Candraens. You are currently located in an underground haven for our people."

"Why don't you just *zap* away and go to another place so they don't capture you?" Tucker asked.

"It's not that simple," said Samuil. "Kiverus has created an instrument that paralyzes our ability. It is very small, golden in color, and can't be seen until the flash is released. Once the flash is released, we are unable to travel. The prisons he created have this same light, which in turn, keep the prisoners from being able to… *zap* away, as you call it."

"So this guy Kiverus is just like a giant bully or something? You guys are going to just continue to hide?" Tucker asked.

Tucker thought they sounded cowardly until it occurred to him how much he had in common with them. He couldn't judge them for responding to Kiverus the same way he did to Dane.

Aeacus spoke up with great emotion and rage, "It is hardly justifiable to compare The Cursed Demon of Xaerdonia to one of your bullies. We have been watching you for some time now, and we know what you consider persecution. This is unlike anything you have ever dealt with in your limited world. Kiverus is wicked. He is beyond evil, and there are no words that can describe his vileness. He has no mercy for anyone, especially Candraens. He has murdered all ages of us, including women and children. He has used the powers that were entrusted to the Lathiaens, and has slowly begun to destroy the worlds. Not just *our* world, but *your* world as well."

Lucan placed his hand on Aeacus's shoulder as if to calm him.

Lucan spoke in a much calmer voice, "There is a Lathiaen blessed with a special gift. He has a power inside of him that can destroy Kiverus. We have been fervently searching for him in hopes he will deliver our people from torment, imprisonment, and... worse. Kiverus and his followers have been searching for him almost fifteen years with plans of destroying him before he realizes his extraordinary powers."

"And you thought this Lathiaen was *ME*? Oh man, you guys were *way* off," Tucker said.

"That has become obvious," Samuil replied with irritation in his voice.

"So, what were you looking for on my hand?" Tucker asked.

Samuil answered, "Candraens have a special marking that appears on their hand when they come in contact with another Candraen. It is called a *veranum*."

Samuil stood up and held out his hand. Marik stepped forward and smiled as though he was about to reveal a secret.

"You may want to come and get a closer look at this," Marik said to Tucker.

Tucker stood up and watched as Marik placed his hand on top of Samuil's. It was amazing. Within seconds, the veranum was revealed on Marik's hand. It was in the shape of a crescent moon and had a mystifying bluish glow that was fascinating.

Marik enjoyed seeing the amazement on Tucker's face.

"Candraens reveal a crescent moon on their hands. Lathiaens have a different veranum and it is located on their right hands instead of their left. Their veranum reveals a unique sun with a yellow glow instead of the blue colored moon that we have. The one we are looking for, the one that will save us, has a truly unique veranum on the back of his neck. We knew we had the wrong person when you didn't reveal either."

Tucker kept one eye on Caedmius from the moment they entered the room. His own amazement over the veranum distracted him. Caedmius had been drawing in the dirt with a stick. Tucker thought the old man was just occupying himself with mindless doodling considering his eyes never once turned from Tucker's face. Tucker looked closer look at the scribble. He recognized it, but couldn't remember from where.

"HEY!" he shouted suddenly, "What is that?" Tucker asked.

Tucker pointed toward the ground in front of Caedmius.

"What are you talking about?" asked Marik.

"The writing… I recognize that writing," Tucker said.

"Impossible. It is a writing that has only been used by Lathiaens and Candraens. It has never been used in your world," Marik said.

"But I *have* seen it," Tucker thought harder and remembered, "I saw it in a book that my friend found in the library!"

"A book?" Samuil asked.

"It can't be. Can it?" Marik confusingly asked Samuil.

All eyes were centered on Tucker, "I swear! I wouldn't lie. We couldn't translate any of it."

Tucker concentrated harder.

"In fact, the pictures that I saw, of the men, and the light and wind, was that you guys? The Candraens? And the symbol on the front, it was part of a sun. Was that the Lathiaen veranum?"

The room filled with intensity.

"This is very important, Tucker! Where is the book now?" Marik asked.

Tucker's voice drifted, "It had five symbols below the sun."

It became clearer now. They were the same five symbols that Caedmius had drawn in the dirt.

"Tucker!" Marik yelled, "I need to know where the book is now!"

"Um, I suppose it's at my friend's house," Tucker offered.

Aeacus spoke with a frightening firm tone, "Marik! Don't be stupid. We can't go back. We can't go looking for the book. Kiverus will find us if we do. We have to lay low!"

"But the book is a key in finding him, and it holds the secrets to destroying Kiverus! If the book made its way to him, surely we can also!"

Marik became very passionate in his pleas.

"Samuil? Can I go? I know I can find him this time. I know-"

Samuil interrupted, "Silence, Marik! Aeacus is right. It is too dangerous now. We know that Kiverus is watching closely. Just be patient. We will think of something."

Tucker may as well have been struck by lightning.

"Ethan?!? You think that the Lathiaen you are searching for is Ethan?"

Samuil replied, "That's enough. Marik, please take our visitor back to his room. We have things we need to discuss. Hurry back when you are done."

"Yes Samuil," Marik said respectfully.

Marik took his hand and pointed toward the hall that had originally led Tucker into the room.

"Come on. Let's go," Marik said to Tucker.

Tucker followed. His thoughts consumed him. Surely his best friend wasn't the Lathiaen they expected would come to save them. Ethan was just an ordinary kid, like himself. Wasn't he? Tucker arrived at his empty room. He sat on the edge of the bed and pondered the whole situation. It was much darker now. The only light came from the glow of the clock. Everything seemed so out of whack, and he couldn't determine what was right and wrong. He guessed they expected him to lie down and "rest" again. This was getting old, and Tucker wanted to go home.

Chapter 9

"Lord Kiverus, my master, I have failed you."

Acharon spoke with intense apprehension in his voice. His body went numb as he anticipated the consequences of his shortcomings. Kiverus remained speechless and motionless adding to the suspense. Acharon dared to raise his eyes from the ground to catch a glimpse of the feet of his master. Kiverus's breathing became louder and more agitated. Panic consumed Acharon's soul as he heard them coming.

"Master? My lord?"

Acharon used the words pleadingly. The howling sound became gradually louder. His heart rate quickened and he was nauseated with fear.

"Please, my lord! I used the device. It had no effect on him!"

Acharon's speech turned into a plea for mercy. With eyes still lowered and body kneeling, he felt Kiverus's presence invading the space between them.

He attempted to sound rational as he continued, "My lord, I have served you for nearly fifteen years and never failed at any task you have given me. This boy is unlike any of the Candraens. My powers would not work on him. He is stronger than you think-"

Kiverus interrupted with great force.

"Silence! He is just a child! He is not special! He has NO powers greater than mine!"

The sounds of howling death filled the sanctuary. Acharon screamed in pain as the demoniacal shadows consumed his body. The other followers swatted the shadows as if to shoo them from the group. Kiverus's mouth curved slightly in the corner as he watched the hysteria taking place. Acharon's cries became fainter as the shadows disappeared with him.

Kiverus's attention focused on the remaining disciples.

"I am LORD! I have proven my power, proven my strength, and no one can surpass me!"

Kiverus's anger provoked fear into all his disciples. They watched as his rage reached heights they had never seen before.

He carelessly took pieces of the elements and slung them throughout the sanctuary.

"I will be DAMNED if this CHILD thinks he can come and take MY throne from me! This is MY world! ALL the worlds are MINE!"

Kiverus let out a growl of intense anger and frustration as he walked toward the center of the temple where the time constituents were positioned. Each one contained the sand vital to maintaining the time balance of its assigned world. They were extraordinarily poised as they suspended above the Fountain of Eternity. He pointed his hands towards them and an enormous dark light exploded from his palms. His followers watched in astonishment as Kiverus continued to release his power upon the time holders. Driven by his anger and rage, he persisted until one cracked causing its sand to pour into the dark and blackened water. Whispers broke out among the group.

Kiverus turned to his followers and spoke with an unusually composed voice considering the severity of what he had just done.

"I want this boy brought to me. I don't care if he is dead or alive. He must be brought to ruin if we are to ever reach our goal," he said.

The disciples bowed to him in unison.

A voice came from the crowd, "Lord Kiverus, my liege, we have a new disciple. I have brought him to you today so he may pledge his loyalty to you."

Kiverus's eyes glared over the crowd. They turned a haunting gray color, and his pupils appeared non-existent. He surveyed his followers dressed in black shrouds and faces hidden by darkness. One by one, their eyes began to glow through the blackness as they met their leader's eyes. He stretched out his long, pale, spider-like fingers and pointed to one who remained dark. Kiverus motioned for him to come forward. The new disciple stepped forward from the crowd. His hands shook as he removed the black cover revealing his entire head. He instantly bowed before his new master. He further displayed his devoutness by placing a single kiss on the foot of his lord. Kiverus stretched out his hand and raised the man to standing position. He was satisfied as the veranum revealed itself on the right hand of the disciple confirming the fact he was a Lathiaen.

Kiverus spoke with a whisper, "You have pleased me. Now you will become like the rest by dedicating your soul to mine."

The man closed his eyes as Kiverus placed his fingers on them. Kiverus leaned forward and pressed harder as he brought forth blood and listened to the anguished cries. The blood ran down the man's cheeks and face. Kiverus removed his fingers and the man slowly opened his eyes. They were now the same gray color as the other followers.

Kiverus spoke to the crowd, "This man has given himself to me and to my purpose. His sight has been transformed and he can now unite himself to any of you that he chooses. Remember, I have created this power so we can use it to our advantage. I am a part of each of you now. I can see through your eyes as well as my own, therefore I can command your thoughts and actions when necessary."

Haygon watched the new disciple from the back of the sanctuary. When he felt his eyes return to normal, he snuck out and headed toward the Candraen prison. He had long ago befriended Lord Thalesten, but his friend was currently held prisoner. Thalesten was different from the other prisoners. He was a Lathiaen. Thalesten's wife was a Candraen. Thalesten and his wife, Giana, had been in prison for over fourteen years. He moved quickly not knowing how much time he had. The guards posed no threat since they were used to the Lathiaens' frequent coming and going. Usually they came to collect the Candraen chosen for the weekly execution, but still, no suspicion ever arose. Haygon quickly made his way to Thalesten's cell. The other prisoners immediately noticed the visitor was Haygon, and all gathered at their gates hoping to hear anything he might say.

"I bring good news, my friends," Haygon spoke softly, "Acharon failed in capturing him. Eitan is still alive!"

Lord Thalesten took a sigh of relief, "Thank you, Haygon. You have given our hope a reason to remain."

Haygon heard Giana crying in her cell.

He whispered, "My lady, did you hear me? Eitan is alive! There is no reason to cry."

She answered softly, "Haygon, I have been anxious for so long. Forgive me for allowing my emotions to get the best of me. You bring such glorious news."

Thalesten had many questions. "What happened? Where is Eitan now? Has he found his way to us yet?"

Haygon whispered, "Slow down, my friend. As you know, Kiverus located him correctly. He took his time, as he wanted to be certain. Once he knew, he sent Acharon to collect the boy. Acharon had Eitan cornered in a building. I was able to unite with Acharon like many others, and witnessed the whole thing. Eitan was very shaken by the events, but," Haygon chuckled a little, "let's just say, he definitely discovered his powers."

Thalesten interrupted, "He knows? He used them?"

Haygon replied, "Oh yeah, he used them all right. I think his fear motivated them."

Haygon's face became utterly serious, "The problem is we don't know where he went. It's both good news and bad. Kiverus will have to start searching again, but Eitan is going to be scared and upset when he realizes what happened. He's going to become noticeable no matter where he is. There is a small chance the free Candraens have found him. I informed them of his location, and I believe Marik was also being sent to collect him. If they locate him before Kiverus, all hope can be restored. I'm going to their haven when I leave here to inform the high council of the current events."

"Good work, Haygon. It's wonderful to have you on our side," Thalesten replied.

Haygon looked around to secure his privacy before he spoke further.

"I have some more upsetting news, my friends. In his anger, Kiverus has damaged one of the time holders."

"What happened?" Thalesten asked with concern.

"When Acheron returned and confessed the news of losing Eitan, Kiverus became enraged. He destroyed several elements in the temple. He took power from his hands and released it towards the fountain," his head lowered with grief, "and a time holder was cracked. The sand poured itself out into the water below."

Thalesten was notably worried as he glanced at Haygon, "The time holder- which world did it belong to?"

Haygon reluctantly answered, "It belongs to Eitan's world. Fortunately, Eitan was no longer there. It isn't good for the remainder of that world though. Time is motionless there unless Eitan returns with the power to fix it."

Giana spoke very gently, "The time holders are vital to their individual worlds. Without them, time ceases to exist and the world will be destroyed! The Lathiaens were chosen to guard all balances of the worlds. This could cause greater damage…" her voice more panicked, "…He's going to destroy them all! He wants complete control and isn't going to stop until he gets it. This is not how it was supposed to be."

Haygon's eyes began to burn and he knew others were trying to unite with him.

"I'm sorry. I must leave now. I will visit the Candraen haven as soon as possible and hopefully return with better news," said Haygon.

Haygon placed a blindfold over his eyes and placed his hood back over his head. The guards would be less suspicious if he kept his head low and covered.

"Thank you Haygon, for all that you do. We understand the danger you put yourself in for us," Thalesten said.

Haygon gave Thalesten a hug through the bars of the cell and slowly walked toward the exit of the prison.

Chapter 10

"Eitan."

The voice was faint. I tried to make sense of the events that just occurred. I knew enough to know I fell a great distance. The ground broke my fall and knocked so much wind out me that I was having trouble regaining enough strength to open my eyes. The voice whispered again.

"Eitan. Can you hear me?"

I wanted to answer but the only noise that departed from my body was in the form of a grunting moan. The light tried to invade my eyelids regardless of my overwhelming exhaustion.

A familiar bell sounded. I struggled to bring myself to a sitting position as the numbness gradually left my body. My vision was returning and I recognized where I was. I sat on the sidewalk across the street from my school. I felt my backpack and wondered what day it was. Had I been running late only to trip and fall? I looked down at Tucker's glasses in my hand and instantly remembered what happened at the school with the janitor, or whatever he was. How could it be that I somehow escaped and ended up out front of the school? The fact that people were shuffling into the school puzzled me. Wasn't it still Saturday morning? Still concerned about Tucker, I decided to investigate into the school and see if I could find him.

Everything was dark and eerie. The sky was an unusual shade of murky gray and blue. The trees' color had faded from them. Leaves were wildly blowing and it was very cold, not at all how I remembered it. Approaching the front of the school, I saw Shelby and Megan from a distance. I walked right up to them and they acted as though they didn't know me.

"Megan, what's going on? Why is everyone at school? Isn't it Saturday?" I asked.

Shelby blushed and answered, "Hi. You're sort of cute. Are you new here?"

Shelby's reaction took me by surprise and I took a step back. Shelby wasn't dressed as her glamorous usual self. In fact, she looked a lot more trashy than normal. Besides the fact her layers of make-up doubled, her clothing was skimpy to near non-existent. Her jean skirt had holes in it where holes weren't intended, and her earrings looked as if they were so heavy they were causing her head to be off-balanced.

"Um. Shelby, what's going on? Where's Kallie?" I asked.

"Who's that?" she replied.

"Quit playing. You know who I'm talking about!" I demanded.

Shelby became uncomfortably close and extremely forward with me. I wanted to move but I was taken back by her shocking behavior. The bell sounded and everyone began to move into the school.

Megan leaned in close to my ear and whispered.

"We can ditch if you want. Go on back to my place. My parents are at work."

Her hands groped me, and I pushed away from both of the girls completely stunned. Something was terribly wrong. Assuming it *was* in fact Monday, I headed to my Algebra class. Tucker shared that class with me and maybe I could find some reasoning there. The inside of the school was trashed. Graffiti was on every locker, wall, and even some of the windows. Papers and books were carelessly thrown about the halls. I made my way into Mr. Neils' class and took my seat. He looked at me as though he had never seen me before.

"Can I help you, Son?" he asked.

"Mr. Neils, have you seen Tucker yet?" I replied.

Mr. Neils looked very confused, "Are you new?" he asked. "Have you checked into the office yet?"

I couldn't believe it! This had to be some sort of prank. Why were they all acting as if they didn't know me?

"You need to go to the office and they will place you in a class." Mr. Neils offered as he pointed toward the door, "The office is at the end of the hall on the left."

I grabbed my backpack hastily and left the room. I wasn't sure *where* I was going, but I honestly didn't want to sit in Algebra today anyway. I headed in the direction of the office, but very unsure as to why. Dane Ivey ran past me so fast he nearly knocked me over in the process. Fortunately, I moved out of the way in time to keep being trampled from a herd of very large

football players. Dane ran into a classroom, turned back towards
them and stuck his tongue out at them. Besides the fact that it
was completely juvenile, I wondered why they were chasing him to
begin with. They vulgarly discussed how they would "teach him
respect after lunch." As if it couldn't get any stranger, Tucker
came around the corner by the water fountain.

 I screamed like a lost child in a department store.
 "Tucker!"

 I was so excited and relieved to see him. I ran at full
speed and nearly couldn't stop. Without hesitation, I gave him a
hug and told him that I was glad he was okay. He pushed me
away and looked at me like I was an idiot. Tears tried to form.

 "Tucker, please don't do this. I get it. It's a joke. I've been
worried about you, and I can't take much more. I'm about to go
insane. Please tell me what is going on!"

 He looked perturbed to say the least, "Dude. I have no
idea who you are, and I'm sorry you are having a bad day but I
need to get to class." He just walked away, "Sorry."

 Tucker was very sincere in not knowing who I was. I just
couldn't understand. I couldn't have amnesia because it was
everyone else who didn't know who I was. I knew it had
something to do with what happened at school earlier with the
janitor. I couldn't imagine how to find answers to this situation.
I've never been one to quit and give up, and I certainly wasn't
going to now. There were answers, and I was determined to
figure this out. I left the school. The frigid outside air seeped

through my skin and chilled my bones. Taking the opportunity to look around at my environment, I realized this wasn't Madison. It couldn't be. I mean, it looked like home, but it wasn't. The neighborhood was significantly more run down. The houses were smaller and most had trash or broken toys cluttered the yard. Several houses even had bars on their windows. The silence broke by two cars yelling profanity at each other from opposite sides of the road. No doubt the talk was about to turn into a physical discussion. There were sirens in the distance, which was definitely a rare sound.

Mrs. Warren came out of the grocery store. She looked much older and aged. She had a cane with her and had a difficult time pushing the cart to her car. Even though she probably wouldn't recognize me, I couldn't help but feel it was my duty to offer some help. I was about twenty feet away from her when a tall man sped past her, grabbed her purse, and darted off. She screamed for help while announcing he stole her purse. Instinctively, I began chasing the man. He turned and ran down a back street. The thoughts of how I was going to handle this if I caught him never entered my mind. Justifying Mrs. Warren was my only concern. I couldn't believe this man took advantage of such a feeble and delicate elderly woman. I followed him down alley after alley and street after street. He turned several times and noticed me following him. Finally, he proceeded down a crowded alley, but disappeared into a building just before I called attention to what he had done. As I turned the corner, people just starred at me. The alley was filled with homeless people. Several large barrels containing burn piles were being used for heat. The surrounding buildings blocked out any sun that attempted to shine. It was very dark and cold. Making my way through the clutter of people, I still searched out my target. He was gone and I was out of breath. I took a seat on some concrete stairs misplaced in the rummage. I was scared. Not so much scared of the people around me, but at that moment, I was terrified about the confirming fact that this was not my home. I had no idea where I was or how to get home. The sounds of shopping carts and babies crying further clouded my attempt at thinking.

I was interrupted by a familiar and soft voice, "Excuse me, but you look kind of lost."

It was Kallie! What was she doing here? She looked as though she hadn't showered in days and she dressed very out of character. Her clothing was way too large and hung on her body in an unflattering manner. I much preferred seeing her in well-fitting jeans and her usual shapely tops. Still, I was so glad to see her. She was always beautiful to me.

"Kallie! I'm so glad to see you!" I exclaimed.

She looked confused. "Do I know you? I don't think we've met before." She blushed. "I'm sure I would have remembered someone like you."

It was par for the course. Not sure why I expected her to recognize me when my best friend didn't.

I mumbled, "I know you, but I guess we've never met before. I hate this!"

"I'm sorry, I'm confused. You think you know me?" she asked.

"I guess I thought I knew you. I know someone that looks identical to you. I sort of *hoped* you were her."

"I'm sorry to disappoint you," she said as she looked around the alley suspiciously and whispered to me. "You know, it isn't exactly safe to be out here alone, especially being a stranger. There are some, who would take advantage of that fact."

I tried to explain I was from a place that looked exactly like the town we were in now; only it wasn't the same place. I only succeeded in adding to her confusion. Her eyes said they tried to understand and she felt badly for me. I became frustrated and angry once again not understanding why this was happening to me.

She took my hand. "I know a man. He's, well… my uncle." She smiled confidently, "Let me take you to him. I think he can help."

She stood up and offered her other hand to help me up. I followed her through the groups of odd people randomly adorning the streets. They mumbled and grunted at us as if to communicate as we walked around them.

We reached an abandoned area and she turned back as she talked to me.

"Please understand my uncle is very protective of me."
She continued with her warning, "He has thoughts and ideas that
are conspiring against everyone. So please don't judge him
quickly. It takes a little while for him to warm up to-"

Before she finished her sentence, a hard blow struck my
backside. I was being attacked. I couldn't see anything and had
no idea who or why this person assaulted me. Kallie screamed for
him to stop. I struggled to get loose, but failed. It didn't seem like
his intent was to hurt me, but definitely prevent me from getting
out of his grip. Disrupting her pleas, she gasped loudly, and the
attacker froze and held his movement. My head was in a position
where I couldn't see his face. In fact, all I saw was the ground.
His hand started to burn on the back of my neck.

Kallie spoke with fright, "Uncle Cayne!"

"I see it, child!" he responded to her.

Almost immediately, he released me and I watched as he
dropped to one knee and bowed before me. His tone was
reverent.

"Please forgive me Prince Eitan. I beg your forgiveness for
I didn't know it was you," he insisted.

I looked toward Kallie. "Are you kidding me?"

Her mouth gaped open in shock. She slowly nodded her
head as to say "no". She was speechless. I was hypnotized by
the brilliant light protruding from her uncle's left hand. It was the
most marvelous color of blue and presented light in the shape of a
crescent moon.

"What... what is that?" I asked.

"My lord? What do you mean?" Cayne responded.

"The light coming from your hand! What the heck is it?" I demanded.

Cayne resumed his standing position.

"You don't know?" he asked in astonishment.

"No! I don't know! I don't know anything, and I don't understand anything! What is going on?" I yelled.

Cayne became frantic.

"Forgive me, my prince, but we must get out of sight. I fear you may be in grave danger and unaware of the weight the situation holds. Please, follow me inside," he said as he gently pushed me.

Cayne entered a building through a rustic fence gate intended to block the door.

"Hurry, please hurry," he whispered to us.

We entered a dark room. Cayne lit a few candles and offered a chair to me. I sat down and saw a mirror hanging across the room. It was at such an angle I caught a reflection of the back of my head off the mirror positioned behind me. A dim light projected from the backside of my neck. I immediately took my hands and touched it to verify its presence. It was very warm and there was no doubt that it was real. Cayne lit a candle close to me and picked up on my new discovery.

"Don't tell me this is the first time you've ever seen that?" Cayne asked.

"I've *never* seen this before. What is it?" I asked while rubbing the warm spot.

"It's called a veranum." He hesitated, "But yours is truly unique and magnificent."

He told me to watch in the mirror as he placed his, now barely glowing, hand over the top of my marking. A radiant light burst forth from his hand with enormous power. When he removed his hand, I could see the image forming from the light on my own neck. It was in the shape of a sun combined with a crescent moon. My neck beamed with an eminent green light. I was amazed.

Cayne was in shock himself.

"I knew it was different, but I didn't expect it to be green. It's fascinating," he said.

Kallie hadn't said a word since it first appeared outside. She poured herself a drink of water from a dirty pitcher and remained silent from across the room. Cayne gathered his composure and sat down in front of me.

"I fear your life is in danger, my lord. It is imperative that I take you to a secret place of my people," Cayne said.

"Your people?" I asked.

"Yes. I am a member of a group of people known as the Candraens. It was long ago prophesied that the chosen child would come to unite the two nations, to save our people, and to restore order in Xaerdonia. It was spoken, the chosen one was given a unique gift that enabled him to fulfill this destiny," Cayne replied. "You are the chosen one we have been waiting for. You are the one deemed worthy to accomplish the tasks that lay before you."

Oddly enough, I felt comfort in knowing there were answers to the insanity I'd been attempting to deal with. There was so much more I still needed answers to, but it felt wonderful to learn I wasn't crazy and grasping the truth was about to become reachable.

"So, if I'm not in Madison, where exactly am I?" I asked. "How come no one recognizes me?"

Cayne's expression reflected his complicated thoughts.

"I'm afraid I am not the best one to be able to explain the elaborate details pertaining to the functions of the different worlds," he said.

He sighed and searched the room. He found a bowl, poured some water into it, and brought it to me.

"Look at the water. You see your reflection," he said as he held the candle light a little closer to me. "With more light, the reflection becomes clearer." He scooped up some dirt from the ground and added it to the water, "When I add impurities to the water, your reflection becomes darker, yet it remains. It is also this way in the different worlds. They are reflections of one another. Xaerdonia is the place that provides light to the different worlds. In recent times, Xaerdonia has become very dark. The mortals inhabiting these worlds mirror each other. They look the same, have some qualities the same, but they in fact, have different souls. They are *not* the same. The actual buildings and surroundings reflect themselves also, making places seem very similar. Yet as you learned, they are indeed very different. Some worlds have more light, and some have more darkness.

My people, the Candraens, are different. Therefore we do not hold this reflection. Neither do you, my lord. This reflection was reserved for only the mortals. It is to their benefit they do not realize these truths, and more importantly, that they never encounter one of their reflections."

I turned toward Kallie. "I guess that explains you, huh?"

I couldn't even fathom the fact I wasn't *mortal*. I suppose it was impossible for me to be with her no matter which world I was in. Kallie wouldn't make eye contact with me.

She spoke as she peered down into her glass.

"I guess it *does* explain a few things. I had no idea I would stumble across a prince today," she said.

Cayne continued, "Unfortunately, the place that balances the light and darkness for the worlds, Xaerdonia, is being destroyed by a wicked ruler. Lord Kiverus has taken unrighteous leadership of Xaerdonia, and you are the one chosen to bring his lordship to end."

There was a loud rumble of thunder and the building shook. Large gusts of wind beat on the outside of the building. Cayne became frantic once again.

"Prince Eitan, we must hurry. I need to take you to the Candraen high council. They will know better how to guide you on your journey," he said.

Kallie interrupted, "I want to go Uncle Cayne!"

"No! It is too dangerous. You must stay here!" he demanded in return.

"I am the one that found him! He is going to change everything and I want to be a part of it!" Her voice quivered as tears filled her eyes, and she said, "I want to do this. I want to be a part of something bigger-"

"I said no! It wasn't a suggestion. You will remain!"

Cayne gently brushed her cheek with his hand, and said, "I love you, my dear niece. While you are in my care, I will make sure you are kept safe. I'm sorry, my love, you must remain here. I will return as soon as I can."

Kallie walked over to me and kissed me on the cheek as a tear from her eye dropped onto my cheek. The thunder was so loud it was difficult to hear anything, but when her lips touched my cheek, the world ceased to exist and all time stood still. It may not have been the Kallie I knew from Madison, but she was close enough for my heart to savor every second.

"Be careful, my prince. I pray we meet again," she turned and walked away.

Cayne touched her shoulder and once again assured her he would return quickly.

He turned to me, "Come Prince Eitan, let me take you somewhere safe."

He placed his hand on my shoulder, and just as it happened in the school, there was a huge flash of light and it was as if we were swept away in a whirlwind.

Chapter 11

Thankfully, the landing was much smoother this time. Just as Kallie's face faded with the bright light, it was Tucker's face I saw when the light faded. He looked rough, but it didn't stop him from showing excitement to see me. He nearly knocked me off my feet while trying to give me an emotional welcoming.

"Ethan! I can't believe you're here! I've been going crazy wondering what all was happening in the *real* world!" Tucker exclaimed.

I was excited to see him also.

"Tucker dude, I have looked and looked for you! And here you are, hanging with some *Candraens* in some strange world! I can't believe I didn't look here first," I said with delightful sarcasm.

"So you know?" Tucker asked curiously.

"Know what exactly? That I'm the chosen one who is going to change the worlds?" I sighed shocked from the reality of my own statement, "Something like that?"

"They say you are a prince or something," Tucker said with astonishment.

Cayne placed his hand on the back of my neck and I felt the warmth again. The light was so bright I saw its shine from the corner of my eyes. Everyone in the room dropped to one knee in front of me.

Tucker looked as though he needed help breathing, "Ethan. Dude, um... well... that's new."

A man stood, "Prince Eitan, welcome. We are honored that you are here. We've been hoping that you would find your way to us," he said.

I looked at Tucker with disbelief. Everything still felt like a dream and I was waiting to be awakened.

Tucker said, "His name is Marik, he's cool," and then smiled.

"Forgive my urgency, Prince Eitan, but the high council needs to see you as soon as possible. Please follow me this way," he pointed toward a long hall.

Cayne, with reverence, bowed his head and wished me luck.

I wanted to send a message with him. "Tell Kallie-"

He interrupted me, "Your majesty, tell her yourself the next time you see her. Let love be your inspiration if need be. All worlds are dependent upon your success. I'm sure you will see her again. If not in one world, another."

I nodded and followed Marik to meet the high council. Several men gathered in a tiny candlelit room. One in particular drew my attention immediately. He was the oldest one there. There was something very familiar and comforting in his aged eyes. Although his mouth showed no emotion at all, I saw joy in his eyes.

Tucker whispered to me, "That old one freaks me out. He just stares, he never speaks. His name is Caedmius."

At that moment, the old man approached me, "You are Eitan?" he asked.

"I have always known my name to be Ethan, but yes sir, I have been told that I am Eitan."

The next thing I knew, he lunged for me and embraced me in a tight hug. I could hardly move.

"Um, yeah. I guess I was wrong again, dude," Tucker said.

When he finally released me, he looked closely at my face and I saw tears forming in his eyes.

"I have waited so long to meet you, my dear Prince Eitan. You have your mother's eyes," he chuckled with a joyous laughter. "You are perfect! You have no idea of the great importance you are to all of us, to me!" he exclaimed.

"I don't understand what it is I am expected to do sir," I said.

"Your friend has told us about a book that has found its way to you. Do you have it with you?" he asked.

"A book? Oh yeah, the book from the library…"

I took the book out of my backpack and held it out to him. His hand caressed the cover. He mumbled some words in a language I didn't understand. Any fragments on the cover were cleared as his hand passed over it. For the first time, I saw clearly the symbol on the front. And even more surprisingly, I recognized it. It was the same symbol that appeared on the back of my neck.

"This is the symbol of your veranum, young prince," Caedmius said.

"Veranum?" I asked.

"Yes, your marking. It appears as a glorious sun with a delicate crescent moon inside of it. It represents the uniting of the two nations. It confirms your destiny in joining them together," he answered.

"What does the book say? Does it tell me how I am supposed to accomplish these things?" I asked.

Caedmius handed the book back to me, "Unfortunately, I can only understand bits and pieces of it. It is written partly in a language that is not mine. It possesses a mystical lock that can only be opened by its owner. It holds the answers you seek about who you are, and how you came to be. It will guide you in knowledge for your tasks. Most importantly, it holds directions that will lead you to the Sacred Armor. This armor is the key to defeating Kiverus. Victory is impossible without it."

Marik spoke up, "Prince Eitan, the Candraen nation is at your command. We are gathering our warriors from all parts of this world and the next. Lord Kiverus took a power that did not belong to him. He used it to create darkness and destruction in all the worlds. He created an army of disciples from his fellow Lathiaens. The ones that have chosen his darkness and wicked leadership have also given themselves to him. He took pieces of his evil soul and penetrated their souls. He has the ability to control their thoughts and actions. And since he inhibits them all, they can become "one" whenever they choose. When they choose to unite with each other, their eyes turn to an empty and wicked gray color. It is then they are all able to see the same things, just as if they were looking out of only one pair of eyes. This is his ultimate army." Marik lowered his voice, "This is how he plans to destroy it all."

"I've seen those eyes before," I said. "a couple of times, actually. They looked at me as though they could see through to the soul of my being."

Caedmius seemed relieved, "We are so glad you found us. We knew that Kiverus was getting close to finding you. We've been searching for so long. You had a guardian named Raedan for the first half of your life. But, several years ago he learned Kiverus's disciples were getting close to him, and you. He had no choice but to leave you, and to his misfortune and ours, he was captured. He successfully led them in the wrong direction for several years before he was captured. He refused to tell anyone, even us, where you were. He remained faithful to his promise of protection for you. He is the most high friend to our queen, your mother."

At that moment I realized how much I wasn't aware of. My mother? I've only known one woman as my mother, and I wasn't sure I wanted it any other way. I suppose it made sense that if I was a prince in another world, that my father and mother must also be royalty to these worlds.

"Where is my mother now?" I asked.

Caedmius became very distant and took a nearby seat.

Marik answered, "She is being held captive in a place that is heavily guarded. A light controlled by Kiverus prevents her escape. Your father and mother have been in prison for nearly fifteen years now. They have also been waiting for your return to Xaerdonia. Their freedom is another that rests upon your shoulders."

I looked at the book. The cover had so much detail that wasn't seen before. I flipped through the book, but didn't understand any of it.

"How do I unlock it?" I asked.

Marik looked confused, "I assumed you would know. But I see that you do not."

I looked around the room for someone to help me know how to unlock its secrets, but everyone looked further disappointed and frustrated.

"I'm sorry," I said.

Caedmius let out a frustrated sigh and suggested Tucker and I go sit with the book. He hoped I would figure it out on my own, but I honestly didn't even know where to begin. How could I possibly unlock something that had no visible lock on it? There was silence between Tucker and I as we sat there looking at an unsolvable puzzle.

Several hours had gone by when someone new entered the room. There was a great conflict of emotions between people when the stranger arrived. Most of the high council greeted him with delight. Caedmius, however, had an apparently reserved spirit about the stranger. His name was Haygon. He dressed much different from the others, and didn't appear to be a Candraen. He told the council that a man named Acharon failed in capturing the prince. I suppose he was referring to me. He stopped in mid conversation and his eyes met mine with great focus.

He grinned suspiciously to them as he said, "Acharon may have failed, but I see you have not! Congratulations, Candraens!"

Haygon's eyes narrowed as he looked intently at me. He had such a different response from everyone else, which in turn, left me feeling awkward. I expected the usual knee bowed and reverent speech, none of which he offered. It was as if he was evaluating me, questioning me.

He turned back to the high council, "Was he able to unlock the book?"

Marik answered with a simple, "No."

Haygon walked towards me.

Tucker whispered, "Maybe it's just me, but I don't like this guy."

"Welcome Prince Eitan. You've had many people searching considerable distances and over great lengths of time to find you. My name is Haygon, and I am at your service."

With that being said, he took his knee and bowed his head to me.

When his eyes looked at me once again, he asked, "Do you have any idea, young prince, as to why you are here?"

I remained silent.

He continued, "I see you have this book of great secrets and information. You don't know how to unlock it?"

"No I don't. I've tried everything I can think of," I replied.

Haygon stood, and within seconds, snatched my right hand and held it in front of him. Caedmius became angry and spoke violently in a strange language. Marik and the others held Caedmius keeping him from reaching Haygon and myself. Tucker was overtaken with concern. I was frightened as Haygon's grip tightened bringing me to a standing position. Haygon grabbed a dagger from his belt and quickly pierced my hand causing blood to flow from my palm. Caedmius was released and the others drew swords of their own.

"Haygon! What in hell's name do you think you are doing?" Marik shouted.

Haygon took my hand and allowed my blood to drip over the cover of the book. The cover of the book transformed itself. The symbol raised into the air and was radiating with a magnificent green light.

Haygon spoke with great intensity, "Now you have unlocked it. Your blood was the key. It would not have opened for anyone, or anything, except for you. You have a special gift that runs deep within your blood. Your blood alone has the power to do great and mighty things, soon you will understand. Please know that your responsibilities and duties are about to present themselves to you. You must grasp that this is not a choice, it is a decree issued to you long ago. It is of significant importance that you are victorious over these heavy burdens. Everything depends on you and your success."

Haygon put the dagger away and his hand returned with a blindfold. He placed it over his eyes and without a word he left the room. Caedmius patted my shoulder as if to express congratulations to unlocking the book.

"What's the deal with the blindfold and him leaving all mysterious?" I asked Caedmius.

He answered, "Haygon is a Lathiaen. He pledged himself to Lord Kiverus many years ago in order to gain information that would help the Candraen and fellow Lathiaen warriors not yet turned. He protects us by putting the blindfold on when he feels the other disciples trying to unite with his vision."

Tucker wasn't satisfied with the explanation. "Aren't you concerned in the least that he can't be trusted? You guys allow him in here? With Ethan here? Haven't you considered maybe he's just gathering information for his wicked leader!"

"I don't like it either, but the council voted and determined, through time, Haygon proved he can be trusted. They've decided it is in our best interest to have him on our side," Caedmius answered.

Marik interjected his own thoughts. "Sometimes, my friend, we must learn to trust others even when we don't know how, and reason isn't clear. Haygon has helped the Candraens repeatedly throughout the years. He has proven to us that he can be of great value."

"I still don't like it," Tucker retorted.

"If it's all right, I'd like to go somewhere alone so I can concentrate on understanding the things held within this book," I said.

Marik looked at Tucker, and Tucker answered, "Come on dude. I'll show you where they expect us to sleep and rest. It's quiet back there."

Tucker led the way and I followed.

Chapter 12

Tucker led me to a doorway and pointed to the bed in the room.

"This is where they told me to sleep last night, although I didn't get much rest," Tucker said.

The room was oddly unfurnished. I suppose for a hideout, one didn't need much in the area of furnishings, but I still expected to see more than a bed. I sat on the edge of it as Tucker said he was going to find us something to eat. I waited for him to leave and noticed the green glow still dimly showing on the cover of the book. I opened the book and flipped through the pages, but couldn't understand it any more than earlier. My hand was still leaking blood sporadically. I took my finger and touched the cut placing fresh blood on one of the pages. An explosion happened causing me to drop the book onto the floor. An image of a hand literally came crawling out of the pages. The hand reached down into the book and returned with a fountain pen. It was amazing how the images were coming straight out of the book. The hand took a position hovering several inches above the book where it spun the pen in a mystical circle causing ink to leak all over the pages, rendering them completely unreadable. I moved from the bed to sit on the floor where I could see better. The spilled ink gathered itself and formed what looked like a small pool of water. I was further intrigued when a second hand appeared from out of the inky water. The first hand continued in a motion as if it was creating a magnificent drawing. The right hand, reached down into the strange ink lifting out yet another hand, apparently the left hand. The right and left hand embraced each other and danced together while the first hand, spinning the pen, dictated their every move. I suppose for being in a strange world, with a strange book, foretelling a strange destiny; this was fitting. The two came together in a tight grasp and the left hand revealed the Candraen veranum while the right hand revealed the Lathiaen veranum. The blue and yellow lights were truly amazing to watch. The hands separated and a small sphere grew between them. The sphere grew and grew until both hands were equally balancing its weight while holding it up. It suspended in the air on its own, but the hands remained, channeling strength in order to continue its floating.   More ink dripped from the pen. This time onto the sphere. The sphere spun and I saw people and places drawn upon its surface.

I heard a very distant voice, but it quickly became clearer.

"Listen closely dear Eitan and we will reveal the unknown you seek. We are the Kruathans, and are the ones that have created everything you've ever seen."

The sphere illustrated the visions described by the voice.

"It began thousands of years ago when we created the Lathiaen people. For centuries, we watched as the Lathiaens strived to please us and gain our praise. In return for their love and faithfulness, we placed honorable duties among them and allowed them to rule over our beloved Xaerdonia. We built them a glorious temple residing in the center of Xaerdonia surrounded by a splendid garden of trees, flowers, and perfect beauty. Within this temple is a fountain containing pure and perfect water vital to the other worlds. The water flows from the fountain into the garden where it nurtures and waters the trees representing the different worlds. The Lathiaen King resides in the temple with his family while he ascertains his responsibilities in caring for the garden."

The pen drew the great willow tree I had visited so many times in my dreams.

"I've seen that tree before," I said.

The voice answered, "Yes, we know. The tree you've seen in your dreams represents all of Xaerdonia. It is through the tree that we have been able to speak with you many times before. As much as we loved the Lathiaen people, we knew there would come a time, as with all nations, they would fail and fall. They were entrusted to help care for the mortal worlds. While visiting one of the mortal worlds, a Lathiaen took a mortal wife and had a child, which created the Candraen nation. This act was against the law, and the Lathiaen King banished the guilty along with his new family. He also created a law that would not allow any Candraen to enter into the Xaerdonia temple."

There was a vision of a man and woman being drawn as I heard the voice speak further.

"Armon was a righteous Lathiaen king. He found the love of a virtuous woman named Ceana. They were married and ruled Xaerdonia in peace for many years. Despite the peace that was in Xaerdonia, much strife remained between the two nations. We revealed a prophecy through the great willow tree predicting it would be Armon's lineage that would bring forth a child who would unite the Lathiaen and Candraen people once and for all. This way, they could carry out our commands and wishes in peace amongst each other. The child would possess a veranum unlike any seen before. Ceana soon became pregnant and their hopes filled with joy in anticipation of the things to come."

The sphere continued to spin and Ceana's stomach grew with child. The scenes showed Armon helping her through the garden as she walked toward the temple. My attention was drawn toward the Cypress tree they walked past and the ground below the tree. On one side, the tree roots were completely buried below the water. On the other side were many rocks and roots above the ground growing toward the temple. Armon gently helped her climb over each root. The voice was silent as the first hand drew meticulously. I examined the rocks a little closer and noticed a tiny solid black scorpion emerge from the ground. There was a black shadow that illuminated everywhere it crawled. The rocks, the roots, and every part of the ground became black as coal when the scorpion came in contact with it. It moved quickly toward the couple. I wanted to warn them to beware, but I knew it wouldn't have done any good. The malicious creature climbed over the top of Ceana's sandal, up her ankle, and disappeared under her long white skirt. I was able to follow it because her beautiful dress turned black wherever it went. The darkness crept to the back of her calf and she let out a frightening scream as she fell to the ground. Armon was frantic as he searched for what was causing her pain. When he lifted the dress from her leg, the black scorpion was still injecting her with its venom. Instinctively, Armon peeled the creature from her leg and launched it into the distance. Ceana still screamed with pain and pulled at her leg. Armon's expression turned to pure fear when he looked at her leg and noticed the veins in her leg were turning black. He picked her up and immediately carried her and his unborn child back to the temple. Although the black in her leg was small at first, the last few months of pregnancy brought greater illness and further darkening of her veins. Ceana repeatedly told Armon she felt the darkness affecting the baby, and she felt something wrong inside.

The voice continued, "The Lathiaen priest visited many times with attempts in alleviating the pain and circumstances, but failed with each visit. The child was expected to be born in the beginning of October. Instead, time continued along with her condition worsening."

The sphere showed a full moon colored a bizarre orange and yellow.

"It was this night that the child was finally born. Within seconds of birth, Ceana's pain was gone instantaneously and her veins returned to normal color as if they were never blackened.

The new parents were further confused when they noticed their new arrival didn't possess the Lathiaen veranum. They presented him to the great willow tree with expectations of answers. The only answer they received was that the child's name is to be called Kiverus."

The voice became solemn, "They had hoped the veranum would later appear, but it didn't. As a child, Kiverus preferred time by himself and away from the temple. He was often caught playing near the forbidden cypress tree, which resulted in punishment. Ceana would've been overly irate if she'd known that Kiverus befriended a tiny black scorpion while exploring his play grounds. It was soon after, Ceana and Armon became unexpectedly pregnant with another child. Around the age of five, Kiverus expressed hatred and jealousy toward his unborn sibling. Great joy was spread throughout the Lathiaen people on behalf of the new prince born at the beginning of October. Kiverus remembered hearing how this child would bless the nations and worlds. The anger rose inside of him.

He watched from around the corner as his mother cradled the new baby and held its hand. Kiverus was outraged when the baby displayed the Lathiaen veranum he had longed for. He wanted more than anything to make his parents proud and to fulfill whatever destiny they had in store for him. Yet, time and time again, he continued to make bad decisions and fail them."

The voice continued,

"You need to understand Eitan, Kiverus not only blamed himself and his parents, but he also blamed us. He questioned us constantly demanding to know the reason we did not bless him with a veranum. He took it very hard and vowed to destroy, not only his parents, but us and everything we ever created. We allowed Kiverus to remain in Xaerdonia with his parents in hopes they could soften his heart. Never allowing his powers to develop only further enraged him. When he would leave Xaerdonia, Candraens taunted him about how he was different. His hatred for their people grew quickly. One night, Kiverus cornered and challenged a Candraen that was insulting him. Kiverus stole his light, turned it to darkness, and killed him. The light that the Candraen carried inside entered Kiverus's soul as darkness. That is why he recently created an army to destroy the Candraens. Although the darkness he gains from killing them may not be as powerful as the light they once contained, it still powers him. He became greedy with his newfound power, and slaughtered Candraens everywhere he went. He believes that once he gains full power, he will not only have the strength to destroy the worlds we have created, but us also."

"That isn't possible is it?" I asked.

"We've never been faced with this situation before. Surely we could have stopped the darkness much earlier in time, but we hoped for change and the best. The last thing we wanted was to destroy the beautiful things we worked so hard to create," the voice answered.

"Rightfully, Kiverus was next in line to inherit the throne of the Lathiaens. Armon and Ceana agreed that his darkness was too strong and he shouldn't become their heir. They in turn, gave the inheritance of the throne to their second born, Thalesten. Thalesten grew up bringing honor to their family and was deemed a righteous prince. Years later, when the boys were teenagers, Armon made an arrangement with the Candraen king and queen. They agreed that Thalesten and the Candraen princess, Giana, would be married and would have a child that would legitimately join the two nations. That child is you Eitan!"

"My father's name is Thalesten and my mother is Giana?" I asked.

"Yes," the voice continued, "Kiverus's hatred and loathing of the Candraen nation deepened when he realized that a child from both nations would take the throne. He refused to bow to such a child, nor heed to the law of both nations. Thalesten learned of Kiverus's wicked plans to destroy them all, including you, and he banished Kiverus from Xaerdonia. Thalesten and Giana were heavily guarded and protected. Giana became close to her leading protector, and asked him, once the child was born, if he would become the child's personal guardian. Raeden was honored by the notion and sincerely agreed.

Both nations were fully aware you were the child that would end animosity between them. Kiverus knew this meant ruin for his plans of destruction. He nurtured his wicked plans, making it a priority to kill you once you were born. Giana gave birth to you near the great willow tree you've seen so often in your dreams. We spoke through the tree and blessed you with a gift you have yet to discover. You have several powers inherited from your parents. Yet the greatest of these, the one we gave you, holds a power greater than has ever been seen before.

You were just a few weeks old when the ceremony was held naming Thalesten the new Lathiaen king. Small gatherings of people were in the temple garden waiting to see the glorious moment, when Kiverus unexpectedly appeared.

Kiverus created a device that disabled the Lathiaen and Candraen ability to travel to different worlds. He told the crowd he already had you in his possession and was going to slaughter your infant body if Armon didn't bow to him, naming him the new Lathiaen king. Kiverus brought much confusion with him and astounded the people by revealing a child's toy stating he took it from your bed when he took you. Thalesten had no choice but to protect you in whatever manner possible. Armon and Thalesten remembered the prophecy we spoke and the gift we blessed you with. They knew if the nations had any chance of surviving, they must protect you. Armon hesitantly gave over the throne to Kiverus. Raeden arrived and saw what Kiverus had done. He didn't believe what he heard because he had left your side a few moments earlier. He snuck away and returned quickly to the temple where Giana held you. He quickly explained to her what happened and that he needed to take the child and hide him far away from danger. Raeden knew once Kiverus gained the crown, he would enter the temple and destroy them all, regardless of any promises he made. Giana was confused but trusted Raeden with all her heart. She begged him to take care of you as if you were his own child. He promised and in a flash of light, she watched her sweet child disappear into an unknown world with his guardian.

Kiverus invaded the temple only moments after imprisoning everyone at the ceremony. His army of disciples were already larger in number than anyone had expected. Giana cried and begged for help as Kiverus stabbed the bed where you should have been lying. He demanded she tell him where she was hiding you. She answered honestly by saying she didn't know. He promised death would come to her and Thalesten as soon as you were found and killed. Every Lathiaen or Candraen that knew anything of the situation was imprisoned. The remaining Lathiaens and Candraens were told Prince Thalesten, Princess Giana, and their child were unexpectedly killed and this was the reason that Kiverus was pronounced king. This only added further discord between the two nations, each blaming the other."

I couldn't believe that all these things had been happening in another world and all because of me. It still felt so unreal. Even though I didn't know my royal parents, I wanted to help them. I understood the importance of my duties.

"We couldn't leave the nations without hope. We sent a dream to Giana's father letting him know she was still alive along with his grandchild. We told him you were safe, had a guardian with you, and we would direct you home when the time was right. We needed you be able to understand the importance of your tasks and abilities. The nations had great confidence you would soon return. Raeden took you to a world and found worldly parents whom adopted you and raised you as their own. He always stayed nearby in order to keep a close but distant eye on you. His faith and confidence grew thinking that Kiverus would never catch on to where you were. About seven years ago, Raeden realized Kiverus's disciples were coming close to finding you. He felt the only way he could protect you was by leaving you. He led them astray and on a chase lasting several years until he was caught. They imprisoned him, but fortunately never found you."

The hand never drew an image of Raeden, but I pictured him very large and strong. He certainly did his job well if it took them seven years before catching up to him.

"I'm so glad you heard our calling when we spoke to you. This is your heritage and account of how you became the Prince of Xaerdonia. Now that you know where you came from, we must show you what lies ahead upon your treacherous journey."

The hand drew a giant iron door with three locks.

"Behind this door is The Sacred Armor you must wear in the final battle. We have locked it here to keep it safe. Kiverus believes without this armor, you would be unable to defeat him. So he has sent many who have searched for the keys to unlock the door, but have done so failingly. It is now time for the one chosen to wear the armor to do so victoriously. You must unite the two nations and lead them into a triumphant battle against the wickedness that plagues Xaerdonia."

"How do I unite them together if they are busy blaming each other for the deaths of the king and queen?" I asked.

"You are already uniting them, young Eitan. They are busy gathering themselves from the utmost ends of the worlds to join you in this epic battle. Like you, they have much to learn along their journey. Your journey is one that will build many characteristics required of a deserving ruler of Xaerdonia. We will watch you and guide you, but we must make our presence scarce. We will not speak with you in this manner again. You must learn to listen with your heart and we will guide you. You will see a vision soon no one else can see. You will see a beautiful woman named Liora. She will help guide you throughout your journey. She was chosen long ago for this task, and has also been waiting to help the prince. Although you may not always be able to see her, she is always with you. She will help lead you to your first challenge, to find Aletheya. Aletheya holds the first key that you seek. He has guarded the key for many years awaiting your arrival.

It is your destiny to defeat Kiverus. Please do not forget this. It is the very reason you were created in this time and place. The gift you hold inside of you is undefeatable. Guard it closely, trust it."

The hand stopped drawing. The right and left hand gathered the sphere between them where it dissolved. They crawled back into the pages from where they came and the voice spoke its final words.

"It is time for us to leave. Kiverus has sensed our presence with you and he is searching for you now. Remember, we will not leave you, but you must learn to hear the still and quiet voice when it speaks to your heart."

The book pages shuffled and the cover slammed closed. I was startled as Haygon appeared in the doorway. Tucker returned with some food only seconds later.

"What are you doing here?" Tucker asked Haygon.

"I came to see if Prince Eitan had any luck in understanding the location of the three keys," Haygon answered.

"They didn't tell me where the keys were. Only that I needed to find them," I answered.

"*They*? Who are *they*? You were speaking to someone? Who was in here with you?" he asked as he surveyed the room, "I assumed you were reading the book."

Haygon's eyes narrowed and focused.

"I *was* reading the book. Never mind," I said. "I was able to understand the book. Just leave it at that."

Tucker pushed his way past Haygon.

"Tuck, were you able to find us something to eat?" I asked.

"Yeah man," he answered and handed me a plate of great smelling cuisine. It was the closest thing I'd ever tasted to my mom's lasagna. It made me miss her.

Haygon made his presence known again, "I suggest you both get a good night's sleep. I suspect tomorrow will hold many adventures for you. I will let the high council know you have understood the writings in the book."

Haygon left and a beautiful girl appeared with a large stack of blankets. She spoke to Tucker.

"Here are some blankets to keep you both warm. The night is rather chilly around here. I'm sorry I don't have more to offer you, Tucker, but I hope you can make something comfortable to sleep on with these blankets."

"Thank you, Abigeal," Tucker said, appearing smitten with the girl when he answered.

She left the room gracefully.

"I take it you know her?" I asked.

"Yeah, we met earlier," he answered, "and she gave me some sort of healing fruit or something."

"Healing fruit? Were you injured?" I asked.

"No man! Haven't you noticed that my vision is great despite the fact I don't have my glasses on?" he replied.

"Oh yeah! Your glasses!" I said as I felt through my bag for them.

Tucker's hand stopped me.

"Seriously, man, I don't need them anymore," Tucker said as he smiled.

I moved my face a little closer to look deep into his eyes.

"They look the same," I said.

He laughed, "I know, right? I have no idea how it happened, but I'm not complaining about it."

I took a blanket from the pile and suggested we both try to get some rest. I wasn't exactly sure where I was headed, but I knew it was going to be a long journey. Rest was something we both needed.

Chapter 13

It was extremely dark. In fact, it was so dark I couldn't see my hand in front of my face. A tiny light formed from outside the doorway. It was as small as a firefly, but considering the darkness, even something so tiny appeared much larger. It was, however, growing in size. The illumination filled the room. Tucker, amazingly, was sleeping soundly as the light continued to invade the room. The figure of a beautiful woman stood in the doorway. All of the surrounding light gathered itself together and entered the burning flame on the candle she held. She wore a breath taking lavender gown. Her hair was long and flowed as if the wind gently blew it. I smelled a familiar vanilla fragrance. The most intriguing feature- she looked exactly like Kallie.

I walked closer to get a better look and make sure my eyes weren't deceiving me. I wanted to reach out and touch her, but I was unsure of whether or not she was a ghost. Her presence brought such peace and comfort. She didn't speak but I understood exactly what she wanted. She motioned with her hand for me to follow her as she placed a single finger over her lips advising me to do so quietly. I carefully followed her without making a sound. As we neared the end of the hallway, we came to a door. She gave me a secretive smile as she turned the doorknob to open it. I had no idea where we were, but the view was beautiful. I walked through the door and she gently closed it behind her.

I whispered to her, "Where are we?"

She didn't answer with anything except a smile. The grass was the truest green I'd ever seen, and the sky the bluest of blues. She gently sat her candle on the ground and took my hand. We didn't walk very far when I saw a large body of water. The atmosphere became a bit colder. As we neared the edge of the cliff, the wind became even chillier. The water had a thin cover of broken ice adding to the chill of the atmosphere. I looked for answers in the mysterious woman's face, but she still offered no words.

I followed her as she walked along the edge of the cliff. A forest banked alongside the river. The trees looked completely covered in snow, yet instinct told me they weren't. Snow couldn't possibly create such a color. Every branch and every leaf, even the trunks of the trees were a brilliant pure white. As I marveled at the beautiful white forest, something caught my eye. There were two trees standing taller than the others. They were bushier and of a different kind altogether. Most amazingly, in the middle of all the pureness, they gleamed with a radiant purple splendor. They shook as though the wind intended to remove their leaves and suddenly melted together to form an arch. It was truly impressive. The leaves were no longer visible and all branches twisted into an intricate design. It was obvious this arch was the entrance into the forest.

"What is this place?" I asked the woman.

Again, her smile was the only answer. She reached around her neck and removed her necklace. It had a very unusual charm hanging from it. It looked like a large circle pinched in the middle and twisted several times creating an endless flow between the two sides. She offered it to me and the bright light it contained dimmed as I placed it around my own neck. As I tucked it below my shirt, I remembered the keys and the armor I needed to find.

"Is this where I find the first key?" I asked.

She nodded. Her face had impressions of concern and fear. She looked toward the sky as if she heard something. It wasn't long before I heard something myself. Half asleep and half awake, I the voices tumbled around in my head. The woman was gone and I, once again, was surrounded by total darkness.

"Be aware, Eitan. You must be watchful of the threats around you. We have impressed on many hearts to help you, but there are still those desiring nothing more than to harm you. You will have to discern them from each other. They have been sent to deceive you and falsely lead you into danger. Remain alert dear Eitan, and be warned. Danger is ever present!"

The voice diminished into the darkness, and I heard someone breathing. It wasn't me. I felt a very real and dangerous presence, realizing I wasn't alone. I fully awakened when I saw the familiar gray eyes staring at me and hovering over me. Startled, I quickly sat up and caught my breath. There was no one there. I wasn't sure how though. I know what I had seen. I remembered my dream and felt around my neck. The necklace was real. I tried to make sense of what just happened and I noticed light coming from the hallway. Voices were becoming louder as the light grew. They sounded hurried and stressed. I nudged Tucker with my foot. He sat up and tried to gain composure although he was still very much in between sleep and reality. I recognized a member of the high council as the first to enter the room.

"Prince Eitan, I am Lucan. I'm sorry to awaken you in the middle of the night but we believe you are in grave danger. Caedmius has had a vision and believes there are traitors amongst our people. It is imperative that we depart from here immediately."

He pointed to two others that followed him, "This is Simean and Oszkar. Together we have been assigned as your guardians and will accompany you on your journey for protection."

Haygon appeared from out of the shadows. It was strange. I hadn't seen him enter the room.

He interrupted Lucan, "Prince Eitan, have you understood the secrets of the book yet? We need to know where the first key is located."

Still dazed, I remembered the dream I just had. "I saw a white forest," I said.

"The White Forest? Impossible. There is no way through it. Many have tried but the trees have consumed entire bodies.

The few that have entered have never returned. Are you sure?"
Lucan asked.

I nodded my head and Lucan handed both Tucker and me
fur coats.

"If we are indeed headed to The White Forest, you will
need to bundle up," Lucan said, "It is very cold there."

We heard more voices coming and sounding angry.

"Please hurry, time is not on our side." Lucan said.

Haygon spoke to Lucan with urgency, "I know the way.
There is a door at the end of this tunnel. We have traveled
through it before, but there is a secret to its use. Follow me."

Haygon began to lead the way when Lucan hesitated.

Lucan said, "You aren't coming with us, Haygon! You do
not have the authority or permission to do so."

Haygon turned with a determined look on his face, "I know
the way to the door. I know its secrets. You my friend, do not.
Trusting me is your *only* option at this moment."

Haygon disappeared out of the room as Tucker and I stood
waiting.

Lucan glared toward Simean and Oszkar and growled.

"Follow him, quick! They are coming!" he said.

I gathered my backpack and put on the fur coat. I felt the
necklace getting warm beneath my shirt. Tucker and I quickly
followed Simean out of the room and away from all other sound. It
was very dark through the tunnels. Lucan and Oszkar followed
closely behind us. It was strange but I felt the danger invading the

very air we were breathing, just as my dream had warned me. After what felt like miles, we finally arrived at a large iron door. There wasn't a door knob or any visible way of opening it. Haygon took his hand, placed it on the door and it magically opened. For the first time, I saw the Lathiaen veranum on Haygon's hand. It was so bright and yellow, it was amazing. We quickly followed him into the room. Every wall was made of thick iron and metal.

Haygon placed his hand on my shoulder, and said, "It is time you learned to travel, my lord. It is different traveling during the day and traveling at night. Lathiaens can travel during the day undetected, and Candraens can travel at night undetected. You are truly unique from both. Because of your great gifts and power, because you are the chosen one, you project a mighty green light that can be seen in all the worlds when you travel. It is important that we keep your whereabouts as much of a secret as possible. These iron walls will absorb your light and keep it from being seen while we travel to The White Forest."

"The prince is going with me!" demanded Lucan.

He looked at Tucker and instructed him to go with Haygon.

"Can I go with one of the others?" Tucker asked, as he pointed to Simean and Oszkar.

Lucan gave him a strange look and Tucker continued, "I'm sorry, but Haygon freaks me out. No offense, but I don't trust him and you want me to zap away with him?"

Haygon looked perturbed.

"Come here, we must leave now!" he said to Tucker.

A flash of yellow light filled the room and they were gone.

"Your turn," said Lucan. "Just take all your thoughts and energy and focus on The White Forest."

I took a deep breath and closed my eyes. I heard Lucan's instruction, "Visualize the White Forest. Breathe its air. Taste its wind."

Great heat came from my hands. They felt like they were on fire. Lucan placed his hand on my shoulder and like an airplane about to take off, he gave orders that everything was clear and it was time to go. Although my eyes were closed, I saw two quick blue flashes in the room and assumed it was Simean and Oszkar. Instantly, I was on my way. I felt the wind and power just as I had before. It was much more controlled this time. As the ground felt firm beneath my feet again, the light also faded.

There was certainly a dramatic change in the temperature. I saw The White Forest, and amazingly it was more spectacular than my dreams could have envisioned. I looked behind me and noticed the cliffs where I had been standing with Liora only a short time ago. A single candle was perched and burning on a rock near the edge. Its flame was almost hypnotizing until I realized that I didn't see Tucker and Haygon.

"Where is Tucker?" I asked Lucan.

"I'm not sure," Lucan replied.

"Tucker!" I shouted.

"Where is Tucker?" I demanded.

A bright flash boomed only a few feet away and I saw Haygon. I had every intention of strangling him until I saw Tucker hanging onto Haygon's leg. Tucker looked like a scared bear cub hanging onto a tree limb. He was shaking and had his eyes closed so tightly I thought I might have to pry them open.

"Tucker, what happened? Are you ok?" I asked him.

He nodded, but the only sound came from Haygon.

"No way am I taking *him* anywhere again! This is ridiculous!" Haygon exclaimed, as he shook Tucker loose off his leg.

Tucker denied any and all accusations that he thought were about to be made on his fault.

"I didn't do anything! That man is crazy and he was trying to kill me!" Tucker charged.

"Enough!" Lucan demanded, "We have more important things to do now that you are both here!"

The wind blew strongly demanding the attention of all visitors. I surveyed The White Forest trying to determine where the entrance might be.

"Excuse me, Sir Lucan, but how do we enter?" Simean asked.

Lucan looked at me like I was to supply the answer. The wind blew close to the trees now. From out of the ground, grew two very large purple trees. It took only seconds for them to grow as tall as the other trees that must have been there for hundreds of years. The branches of the trees performed a magical dance while intertwining with each other. Once they formed a complete arch, a very distinct pathway was visible. It entered directly into the forest.

"I guess that's how," I said as I pointed out the answer to Simean's question.

I walked toward it as the rest were frozen in amazement.

"Are you coming?" I asked them.

"Heck, yeah! I wouldn't miss this for the world," Tucker answered excitedly.

The remaining four looked at each other in bewilderment and then resumed their task in escorting me to the forest entrance.

Chapter 14

The icicles dangling from the trees sounded like wind chimes blowing in the breeze. Simean and Oszkar hesitated as we neared the purple arch entrance. They reminded Lucan about the stories of warriors entering and never returning. I, on the other hand, was being drawn to enter. I knew this was where I should be, and I knew I had to enter. There was a pathway made of stone just a short distance beyond the entrance. I pointed it out and hoped they would follow my lead. Simean was the last one to enter. As soon as his foot touched the pathway, there was a loud thunder and the entrance closed.

"No turning back now," I said.

We followed the path for quite some time. It was actually much warmer inside the forest than it was on the outside. The trees provided shelter from the outside. As I followed the pathway of stones, my thoughts wandered. I thought about what the book had told me about how my journeys would change me and develop me. I had already begun to change. The events that occurred over the last few days had brought me on such an amazing adventure already. I savored the fact that these were the first official steps on my journey. I had no idea what was in store for me, but I understood the goal. I understood the importance of my success. Tucker was walking right beside me and I saw the excitement on his face. He looked like a child in a winter wonderland, only there wasn't any snow. Everything was just supernaturally white. I wished Kallie could have been there with us. She would've found it beautiful.

The further we walked into the forest, the darker it became. It was still very bright, but not as pure as when we first entered. The path beneath my feet was breaking up. It looked like the stones had been moved, or maybe never even laid. White grass was filling in the gaps between the stones. Simean and Oszkar were also noticing the differences. The stones were now officially pebbles and were so scattered that the pathway appeared non-existent. I had to stop and think. I wasn't sure if we were lost. Maybe I had taken my eyes off the path and lost track of where we were headed. It appeared that we were standing in a large empty field. All the plants were white, even the little butterflies and other flying creatures were white.

"Look," Tucker said.

He pointed to something dark a little further ahead of us. It was a dark tunnel. The closer we went; I saw that there were actually two paths. The whiteness ended at the entrance of these two paths. The flowers were very large and colorful at the entrances. The dew drops on the hibiscus beside me were the size of golf balls. There weren't any clouds, and the sky was hardly visible. So where did the dew come from? It was rather strange and out of place.

My thoughts were interrupted by Lucan.

"So which way do we go, Eitan?" he asked.

"I'm not sure," I replied.

I pulled the book from my bag hoping it may be able to guide us. It was glowing so brightly I had to look away. It was at that moment I noticed the dew drops were moving. They spun in circles and moved around us.

"What do you think this means?" I asked.

"What, what means? Tucker asked.

"The book, the dew. Maybe it's trying to tell us something," I replied, as the dew continued to spin around us.

Tucker, closer to my face, asked, "Dude, seriously? What dew? What about the book?"

"The book is almost blinding me! You don't see it?" I asked Tucker.

"No," he replied, as he looked to the others for answers.

"Doesn't anyone see the book? Can't you see the dew around us?" I asked.

They all looked at me like I was crazy.

Tucker finally responded, "Ethan, maybe the atmosphere is messing with you or something. There's nothing here, dude."

I knew what I saw. I just couldn't figure out why they couldn't see it. Oszkar cut back some bushes and announced there was a sign.

"Look. There's one over here as well," said Simean.

There was writing on them, but none of us were able to translate the words.

"A choice has to be made. We can't stay here forever. Prince Eitan, you must make a decision and we will follow," said Haygon.

I spoke as loudly as I could in my own mind, "Please help me, Liora. If you can hear me, I need you. I need you to guide me. Please."

The voice sounded like a whisper from Kallie. I wasn't sure if I actually heard a whisper in my ear, or if it was just the wind. Regardless, I heard something.

"Follow it. It will guide you," were the words that blew in my ear.

I opened my eyes and the dew was a few feet ahead of me down the pathway to the right.

"This is the way," I said as I began to follow.

Every step I took closer to the dew drops, they moved further away. I felt the uncertainty of my companions. The white that the forest once held was now turned to gray. Normal colors appeared in the plants and trees. The deeper into the forest we went, the darker everything became. My spirit was being dragged down along with those around me. They were all becoming very short with each other and didn't hesitate in sharing their frustrations. It made the sudden light we saw up ahead seem like an oasis in a desert. Again we came to two pathways and the dew drops melted into the light. The climate had become much colder and Tucker was sniffling much more now. The book had been glowing the whole time, but I was the only one that saw it.

The light faded, and I placed it back in my backpack. The pathway to the left was wide open without trees. It was well lit and looked as though it provided a peaceful journey. The pathway to the right looked very dark with lots of trees. Very little light gave the impression of a more treacherous path.

"Well, this is an easy choice," said Oszkar, as he began down the path to the left.

"Thank goodness, it looks much warmer down this way," said Simean, following.

Haygon watched me intently.

"What are you thinking, my lord?" he asked.

"I'm not sure. The path to the left would appear to be the more comfortable choice, but honestly, it just looks too easy. I can't help it, but I'm not sure that it's right," I replied.

"What are you doing? Aren't you coming?" asked Simean.

"Hold it, Simean!" Lucan demanded.

"You have got to be kidding me! This is not a hard choice!" said Oszkar.

"Seriously Haygon, the left does appear to be the best option," Lucan said.

"It is not a choice that is ours to make," replied Haygon.

Tucker's eyes were fixed upon me. I closed my eyes and tried to listen.

"Prince Eitan," said a faint voice.

The arguing between Lucan and Simean was drowning out any thoughts or voices.

"Please stop!" I yelled.

"Eitan." I heard the whisper again, "Prince Eitan, you must learn to trust your heart. This is *your* journey. It is *your* destiny."

The others watched but never heard a thing. I spoke to myself which only further convinced them of my instability.

"I don't know which path to choose," I whispered back.

"Were you guiding me before? Why did you leave?"

"Dear Prince, I haven't left you at all. I am still guiding you, and I am still here with you. You have powers that are greater and mightier than you could ever imagine. You must learn to use the gift inside of you. This is a choice you *must* make alone. You must heed to the nudges of the light inside of you and learn to have faith in it," whispered the voice.

"But which path do I choose?" I asked, and received no reply.

I was frustrated when I didn't get a clear answer from the voice.

"I can't do this alone! I don't know what to do!" I said to the others.

"Please, let's just go this way," Simean said to Lucan as he pointed to the left.

I was about to follow when I felt the wind blow back against me. I took a deep breath and determined to stick with the decision they had made when I caught a whiff of a sickening aroma.

"What is that?" I asked.

"What?" replied Tucker.

"Again? Please tell me you smell that stench!" I said.

Tucker looked around for approval, "No, man. I don't smell a thing."

It was obvious the smell was coming from the path we were about to travel. Even more obvious, was the unmistakable scent of death that the wind carried.

"This is wrong," I said quietly.

"What is?" asked Haygon.

"This path. It's wrong. I know now. We have to go the other way," I replied.

"Prince Eitan, are you certain?" Haygon asked.

I went back to the pathway that led to the right. I only took a few steps when I noticed a ray of dim light shining through the trees. I remembered what the voice said, "the light", and I repeated it out loud.

"We have to follow the light!" I announced.

"What light!" demanded Lucan out of frustration.

"The light is this way!" he said, as he pointed to the path to the left. "Your path only has darkness!" he exclaimed, while he pointed towards the right.

I replied to Lucan, "I understand your aggravation, and for that, I'm sorry. I know we are all in a world that is not our own and with that comes much confusion for us all. You must trust me. If I am indeed the one chosen to bring together these nations and to defeat Kiverus, you must be patient and have faith in me. I'm still learning, but I know I can do this.

Haygon removed his blindfold and placed it over his eyes.

"Darkness seems to beckon to me often. I will follow you Prince Eitan," Haygon said.

Tucker touched my arm as if to show his allegiance.

"Ethan, I have faith in you. I believe you feel you are making the right decision. Honestly, though, I'm looking down this path and I see nothing but darkness. But, I'll follow you if you say you're sure," Tucker said.

"I'm sure," I announced to them all.

And with that same breath, I turned and followed the light that only I could see. Just as before, the closer I became to the light, it moved further away. It looked like search lights shining through the trees creating magnificent rays. It was a shame I was the only one who could see them. I tried to remain focused on light and what lay ahead, but the grumbling from my so called guardians was enough to distract anyone. They were having a hard time seeing in the darkness, and I was grateful I could see the guiding light. It wasn't long before our path, and guidance, came to an abrupt halt. The light disappeared behind a giant wall of trees. The way the trees entangled within one another resembled the arch that was at the entrance. I felt the wall with my hand and confirmed it was strong and solid.

"It may as well be a wall of iron," stated Simean. "There is no way we are getting through that."

I closed my eyes and whispered quietly once again, "I've trusted you this far, and I believe you are leading me in the right direction. I can't see beyond this wall, and I've lost the pathway. I can't see your light or guidance. Please help me once again."

"My dear Eitan, trust yourself. You already have the power within yourself. You followed the light that you saw with your eyes, yet there is a light within yourself that you cannot see. It is more powerful than you know. Trust it. Use it," I heard the voice whisper.

The light inside of me is part of what I was trying to understand. I remembered back to when I was cornered at the school. I felt the power and strength inside of me, but I didn't have any control over it. I also remembered back in the iron room how I used my power to travel to a new world. We needed through this wall, and I was told I had the power. I stood with confidence, at least as much as I could. I closed my eyes, and breathed slowly. I held out my hands and the heat rose in them. The warmth on the back of my neck strengthened me, and light filled the area. Those around me were utterly silent. My hands protruded a powerful light, and I aimed them toward the great wall of trees.

I spoke loud and directed at the wall.

"I am Prince Eitan. I hold a great and powerful light before you. I have been led down a pathway you are now blocking. I command you trees untangle yourselves from one another. Take up every part of yourself including your roots and remove yourselves from here."

There was a deep moaning that came from within the trees. We watched in awe as they fulfilled my request. Each tree became an individual once again. The branches became arms and hands. They literally bent at the truck and with their hands lifted their roots from the ground. Once they began to separate and move, the icy lake appeared behind them. They continued walking until they reached the lake where they released their giant roots into the water. They lined a new path for us that led to the water. Each tree bowed at the trunk as I walked past.

"All of creation knows who you are, Prince Eitan. All creatures, in all of the worlds, are dependant upon you and your success. They are honored to be in your presence," Haygon spoke quietly.

As we neared the water, there was a small boat at the edge. It was waiting just for us.

"Well that's just handy," said Tucker.

"Yeah, sort of convenient, huh?" I replied with a smile.

Simean and Oszkar had very little to say at this point which only made me smile a little more.

"Load up men, our journey awaits us," Lucan said as we all entered the boat.

Chapter 15

We took our seats in the boat, and it was peculiar there weren't any oars. There was absolutely nothing to row the boat with. We sat there looking at each other waiting for someone to get a brilliant idea when the wind knocked the boat loose from the icy shore. As much as it chilled us to the core, it was strong enough to keep the boat in motion. Simean quietly expressed his concern over the fact we also had no way of steering. It was beyond all their comprehension that maybe, just maybe, we were receiving help and guidance even though it couldn't be explained. I felt it best to keep my thoughts to myself.

The sky gradually grew darker again and The White Forest disappeared further and further into the distance. There wasn't much in sight except the large body of water surrounding us. Waves crashed around the boat causing a great deal of nervousness to the other passengers. The water was merciless as every wave jolted the boat. We traveled this way quiet a distance before the waves began to settle. Fog thickened and even the warm breath from our bodies wasn't seen. The boat was led into a much colder and frozen area. The waves lost their power and turned to slushy ice. Edges of the boat now had icicles dangling. The icy water slowly became solid, and ice chips from the wind hit us rigorously. Much like our breathing, the boat was sluggish as it fought its way through the thickening ice.

I sensed we were getting close to wherever the boat was taking us. Suddenly, we crashed into a large block of ice. It was still hard to see because of the thick fog, so it looked like we were surrounded by ice as far as we could see.

"Great!" Simean complained. "So now we are just stuck out in the middle of nowhere, and we are going to freeze to death."

"Be patient, Simean," Haygon said.

"Be patient about what? We followed your *majesty*," Simean directed toward me, "out on a goose chase, and what if he was wrong? There is nothing here except ice! We should have taken the path to the left way back when we were in the forest. This is ridiculous! You are going to allow him to risk all our lives. This is not what I signed up for!"

My heart raced faster and I knew sitting in a stranded boat wasn't the thing we needed to do.

"What is it, Ethan?" Tucker asked.

"Something is wrong," I replied.

"Yeah, something *is* wrong!" Simean interrupted as he stood up in the boat.

"Control yourself, Simean!" Lucan demanded. "You know what you were brought here for! You knew the risks before you were assigned the task. Do your job or I will personally put you out of your misery," Lucan said, as he stood to meet Simean nose to nose.

The danger became increasingly more present.

I looked at Tucker and spoke quietly, "We need to get out of the boat!"

"And go where? We're surrounded by ice," Tucker whispered in return.

"Excuse me, but did you say we need to get out of the boat?" Lucan asked.

"Yes and quickly. It's coming," I answered.

"What's coming?" he asked in return.

"I don't know, but it's trouble."

"Well, in case you haven't noticed, we are surrounded by ice and don't exactly have anywhere to go. If we try to get out of here, our weight will break the ice. How long do you think you can swim in icy water?" Lucan asked.

Suddenly, a violent jolt knocked Simean and Lucan back to a sitting position.

"What the hell was that?" Oszkar asked.

Everyone was silent. Tucker stretched his neck to look over the edge of the boat and into the water to get an answer. I grabbed him back.

"Don't. Get out. We need to get out!" I told him.

Tucker looked at me like he found a new faith in me and agreed completely. The snow fell quickly now. It would be hard to know where to go. I wouldn't be able to accurately lead them without a path, and I had no idea how thin the ice was. A quick survey of the area, and I stood to my feet. Strange bubbles brewed from the water several feet away from us. The others saw my concentrated stare and turned to see for themselves.

"What is that about?" Lucan asked.

"I think we better do as Prince Eitan says and get out of the boat, now!" Haygon replied.

Some of the snowflakes fell with a luminescent color making them stand out from the surrounding snow. They created a pathway. Amazingly, I saw an entrance to a cave in the distance.

"Follow the light," I said.

I stepped my first foot out of the boat creating a deep crack into the surrounding ice. Tucker looked even more terrified.

"Trust me, Tuck, this is right. We need to hurry," I said as I extended my hand to him.

Tucker and I successfully made it out of the boat and moved quickly toward the cave. The others made their way out of the boat also. I didn't turn around to look, but I heard some commotion going on behind us. Tucker looked back and saw Oszkar having trouble getting out of the boat.

"Wait a minute, Ethan!" Tucker said.

Haygon almost caught up to us with Lucan trailing close behind. The ice made it hard for all of us to move quickly as we were sliding as much as running. Simean was moving toward us, but screamed at Oszkar to get out of the boat. The place where the bubbles began now exploded with bubbles. Oszkar gained enough courage to stand and make his way to the edge of the boat. He stepped out onto the ice, only to cause it to crack a little more. This time, the crack made a noise sounding like lightning bursting.

"Bloody hell, hurry up Oszkar!" Simean yelled.

We were close to the entrance of the cave now and Lucan caught up to us.

"We need to go back and help him," said Lucan

"Wait," said Haygon, grabbing Lucan by the arm.

From the center of the lake came a gigantic creature roaring with rage. Oszkar froze with fright even though his back was to the creature.

"Oszkar! Run! What's wrong with you!" Simean screamed.

Oszkar tried to turn to see the creature, but was blinded by his own fear.

"Where is it? I can't see it! Help me! I can't see where you are, Simean!" Oszkar pleaded.

The earth shook again, causing the crack to split a little closer to where Simean stood.

"Timordis," Haygon whispered.

I looked at Haygon confused, "You know what that hideous thing is?"

"Simean! Timordis! Run!" Haygon screamed.

"Run," I said to Tucker.

We ran toward the ice cave as fast as we could. It was hard to keep our footing on the ice. We slid everywhere, but had one destination in mind. The light from inside the cave became brighter.

"Just run, Tuck, don't look back. Run toward the light!" I said in between breaths.

Haygon and Lucan followed close behind us. Oszkar screamed in fear. Once we were safe at the entrance, we turned only to see the giant creature standing at its full height. It was horrifying. It broke through the frozen ice with ease as it moved closer to Oszkar. The louder he screamed, the faster the beast moved towards him. He was dragged below the ice with the monster just as Simean reached us. Within seconds, complete silence once again saturated the air. The water was instantly motionless and quickly refroze.

Simean tried to catch his breath. Lucan was enraged and demanded answers from Haygon.

Haygon answered with a single word, "Timordis."

Simean retorted, "Impossible! Timordis is a fictitious monster created to scare children."

"Well, it scared more than children, and it obviously isn't just fictitious."

Haygon looked to me and further explained. "Timordis is a creature that feeds off of fear and doubt. He lives deep in the depths of mysterious waters. Sailors and fishermen have told stories about this extraordinary monster for centuries. Yet, no one has ever had any proof that such a creature exists." Haygon was very still. "I suppose we should all be grateful we are still here."

We entered what was an almost empty cave. The top of the cave must have been twenty feet up. It had intricate and detailed etching in every corner of the ice. The others were taken with amazement, but I noticed something in the corner of my eye. It looked like a dark tunnel. In front of the tunnel was a podium made of ice covered in green leafy vines. I approached the podium and noticed a tiny sign that was near impossible to read:

RING BELL FOR SERVICE

I looked around and saw the tiny bell sitting to the left of the sign. I reached out and pressed it only to hear a faint "ding". It startled all of us to hear sudden howling and snarling coming from deep within the tunnel.

"Maybe it's just me, but in light of recent events I don't think it's the best idea to enter that tunnel!" Simean said.

"Yes, this is definitely not some place we want to venture into, Prince Eitan. Come, let's go back out and see if we can find another way," Lucan suggested.

"Hang on," I said. "We made it this far, and this bell is here for a reason. Nothing came out to eat us, so let's just see what happens."

I reached out to ring the bell once again, but this time with determination. A much louder chime echoed through the cave. I heard mumbling of some sort, but only saw what looked like a small shadow moving slowly in the darkness of the tunnel.

"Every time. Every. Single. Time. Can't get no sleep up in this place," the voice said.

"Excuse me?" I offered to the voice.

The voice continued with its lengthened complaining. We only heard bits and pieces between grunts.

"Tired…not appreciated…everyone want or need something!"

It was a lizard of some sort, and he wore a black nightcap and gown. He paused in mid stride to take a lengthy stretch before he climbed the vine wrapping the podium. It was easier to see him as he turned from black to green. His nightcap and gown faded and was completely replaced with a miniature white tuxedo. His grumbling stopped. He reached the top of the podium and presented with an unusually fake smile.

"Hola. My name is Rogelio De La Cueva. I am excited for you to be here. How can this chameleon be of service to you?"

Tucker was the first one to respond, and he responded with a loud burst of laughter.

"Dude! Am I dreaming? What the heck *is* that thing?"

The chameleon's smile strained and showed irritation, but remained.

"I said…I am Rogelio De La Cueva. I am happy to be awakened from my warm bed in order to serve you. What do you want?"

Everyone wanted to chuckle at the grouchy little lizard, but we were able to remain composed. Well, everyone except Tucker that is.

"That is so cool! Can you change clothes again? Or color?" Tucker asked with amazement.

The chameleon rolled his eyes, but smiled even larger.

"This is my happy suit. Would you really prefer I change clothes, chico? I be more than happy to do so, if you like."

I replied for Tucker, "No. You are fine as you are. We do require some assistance, though."

He shot his tongue out toward Tucker startling him to silence, and then licked his lips with satisfaction. I noticed Rogelio's first sincere smile of gratification.

"I am looking for a key," I said.

"Ah!"

He climbed to the tallest part of the vine and came very close to my face. All I saw was a giant eyeball rolling around inspecting me. Finally, he spoke once again, "Yes, I can see this. You are especial indeed."

He jumped back with excitement, and said, "Come. Let us see if you are the one we have waited for."

He climbed up my arm and took a place on my shoulder. He pointed the way down the dark entrance to the cave.

"Come. Hurry, this way, señor," he said.

I took a deep breath as howling from the beasts filled the tunnel again. I took a few steps forward when Lucan shouted,

"Wait!"

He tried to reach for me but there was an invisible wall separating us. All of them became panicked as they banged on the wall.

"Stop it! Stop it you stupid locos!" Rogelio demanded. "Only one at a time can enter here. You must wait here for him to return. Many have come here looking for the key of which you speak. None have returned with it yet."

"What happens to them when they don't return? How do they get home?" asked Tucker.

The chameleon formed another strange smile as he spoke.

"They don't return home. Can you not hear the howling?"

His eyes narrowed as he continued, "Those beasts you hear, guard this cave. It has been some time since their last meal."

He smiled awkwardly at Tucker and then spoke hastily to me, "Come. Let us see if you can find your key."

I walked deeper into the dark tunnel.

Rogelio yelled back, "No worries. I will escort him back to you if he survives!"

The voices of complaints faded the further I walked into the darkness.

Rogelio was all that kept me company.

"Keep walking straight. You will not fall," he said.

I whispered quietly, "Liora? Are you still with me?" It was completely silent.

"Who you talking to, Amigo?" Rogelio asked. "I told you already. You are the only one here." Rogelio chuckled to himself, "Except for me. I be with you till we reach the door."

"What door?" I asked.

"That door," Rogelio stretched out his tiny hand and pointed.

I approached the door and examined its intricate detail. There was a message formed within the ice-covered door:

In order to understand truth, you must first understand the lie known as deception.

"What's behind that door, Rogelio?" I asked.

"I do not know," Rogelio answered.

"Haven't you ever been in there?" I asked.

"No. This is where we part. I will wait here for you. Hopefully you will return," said Rogelio. "None of the others have ever come back out. I wish you luck. You are indeed especial."

Rogelio climbed down from my arm and waited anxiously at my feet. I reached for what appeared to be the doorknob only to watch my hand disappear into the door. I immediately pulled it back and looked to Rogelio for answers. He only shrugged his shoulders and smiled. I figured it was all or nothing, so I charged into the door and found myself standing in a curious room.

I stood at the top of a winding staircase. My only option was to follow the steps to the bottom. The ground quaked slightly when I reached the final step, and there were two pillars standing alone in the center of the cave. At the top of each pillar stood a single goblet. The stench of death was overwhelming throughout the cave.

A loud voice spoke from the silence.

"You should not have come here! You are not worthy to receive what you have come for! You misplaced your trust in the chameleon; he has led you to your death!"

"I am Prince Eitan, and I have come-"

The voice spoke with sternness, "Silence! I do not care why you have come! You are now faced with your final decision!"

The ground shook again and an empty skull rolled closer to my feet.

"You see the two goblets. You will choose one of them. You must make one single statement about your choice, and choose wisely what you say. If your statement is the truth, you must drink from the goblet on the left. Its contents will give you a fast and painless death. If your statement is a lie, you must drink from the goblet on the right. Its contents will give you an agonizing and slow death."

I wanted to shout "neither" and run back up the stairs, but when I turned around, the staircase was gone. I remembered what the door had written on it, and I remembered the words of the chameleon. I knew I couldn't trust anything I've seen or heard. It was apparent I was going to have to make a decision about the goblets, though. I knew neither of the two options was what I was promised nor destined to accomplish. My destiny was not going to end here! So I sat and thought. A long time had passed by before it hit me. And when it hit, it struck like lightning.

"I am prepared to choose!" I shouted.

"Make your final statement, then," the voice replied.

I forced the lump in my throat back as I uttered the words.

"I will drink from the goblet on the right, receiving an agonizing and slow death." With those words, I reached out my hand to grab the goblet.

"WAIT!" shouted the voice. "If your statement is the truth, you must drink from the goblet on the left! But if you indeed drink from the goblet on the left, it would make your statement a lie!"

I was so proud of myself.

"It seems that you have chosen wisely, Prince Eitan. Your wise thinking has left me with no choice, but to forbid you to drink either. Drinking from either would break the rules that were placed upon the goblets. You are free to go forward and find Aletheya."

The ground shook and a great crevice formed between the two pillars. As the fissure opened further, another set of stairs appeared. A bright light came forth from out of the ground and I followed it down the stairs.

"Welcome, Prince Eitan," said a deep and strong voice.

When I was able to stop squinting from the light, I saw a very large and tall man standing in front of me. His hair was gray, but his skin was smooth and showed no sign of age.

"Aletheya?" I asked.

"Yes, you have found me. And I have something to give you," he said.

He reached into his pocket and pulled out a key. It was glowing at first. I took it by the loop from which it was hanging and thanked him. He patted me on the shoulder and laughed.

"I thought you would be a little bigger," he said as he continued to laugh. "No problem, though, Prince Eitan. I am sure you will grow along your journeys."

I could hear the faint sound of the howling once again.

"You better hurry back to your friends before they become dinner," he said.

"You will need this, and feel free to share with your friends. You still have a long way to go before you reach the armor," he said as he handed me a large bag, "and remember to always trust your heart."

I turned to walk back up the stairs, but the door of ice was already in front of me. There was nothing but light behind me. I saw Rogelio pacing back and forth in front of the door, and it was obvious he could not see me. I walked back through the door, and Rogelio began to cheer with excitement.

"I knew you was especial! I told you that you was especial!" exclaimed Rogelio. "Come. I take you to your amigos now."

Rogelio quickly climbed up my arm and pointed the way back.

Chapter 16

"I knew it!" shouted Tucker, "I knew you were a traitor!"

I heard them arguing before I even saw them. The tension was great when I rejoined them. I expected a much more joyful reunion, but instead was greeted with tremendous hostility and animosity.

Tucker had such a visible fury.

He pointed to Haygon, and said, "Ethan, he's a traitor! I told you he couldn't be trusted!"

"What's going on?" I asked.

Haygon started to speak, but Tucker interrupted.

"He just admitted that Caedmius didn't give him permission to accompany us. He said that Caedmius specifically commanded him *not* come because there were those who were sent to kill you. Caedmius believed there were ones the Candraen people mistakenly trusted. They were wrong in trusting Haygon, and he knows it!"

"He's right," said Lucan. "Haygon was sent to kill you. We only allowed him to come because he knew the secrets of the Iron Room and was our only way to escape. We were going to address this issue with you once we reached the first key. We didn't know if we would need his help again though."

Haygon tried to reason, "Prince Eitan, my lord, I assure you I am not a traitor. Lucan speaks lies. He is right in saying that Caedmius did not approve of me coming with you, but there is a bigger story than you've heard-"

"Shut up you wicked follower of Kiverus," Simean said, as he restrained Haygon from moving.

Tucker raged, "They are only fighting because of the history between the two nations. I think they were both sent to kill you Ethan!"

"Enough. Release Haygon," I demanded of Simean.

Simean did so reluctantly.

"Please finish what you were saying," I requested of Haygon.

"Your majesty, Caedmius is rightfully suspicious by nature. It isn't a secret that he doesn't trust me. The high council met late last night. They learned there are several of their own Candraen brothers that have conspired against you. These traitors have been offered rewards by Lord Kiverus's disciples if they were to convince you to lead them to the keys. Their only intentions are to gain the keys, the armor, and to destroy you. I snuck into your room before anyone else arrived. I was there to protect you. I wanted to make sure there weren't any deceivers that would get to you."

"Lies!" said Lucan. "You were in his room because you were going to kill him! We interrupted your plans when we unexpectedly rescued him!"

I held my hand to Lucan to silence him.

Haygon continued, "It wasn't until be were in The White Forest I realized the very ones I wanted to protect you from, were the ones I was helping."

"We were sent to protect you, Prince Eitan," Lucan said firmly.

"How do you know they have intentions to harm me?" I asked Haygon.

"I have seen it. It appeared to me when we were walking in The White Forest." Haygon looked bitterly toward Lucan, "You forget when the disciples unite with one another, we can see as one. You may not understand how this works, but let me assure you we see it all, even the betrayal. Lucan, you grew up knowing Caedmius like a father. Yet, you turned your back against your entire nation and betrayed him in the worst way possible!"

Haygon turned toward me again, "Prince Eitan, I know your mother and father. They have been friends of mine for as long as I can remember. I have made the choices I have made with your well-being in mind. I have always sought to protect you, my lord. I gave up parts of my soul in hopes I would be of assistance in keeping you safe, in hopes my services would bring you home quickly. It was the only way I could know what the disciples were planning, and the only way to be able to take vital information to your parents and the Candraen people. Thanks to these two, and some others, I am afraid I cannot return to Lord Kiverus or else he will destroy me for sure. I am not safe anywhere. In fact, I may be putting you in danger unintentionally just by being with you. It would be wise for you to proceed without me."

Haygon took out his blindfold yet again.

Lucan argued, "See, he can't even look at you, Eitan! He is a danger to us all! He is a disciple of Lord Kiverus and they are all programmed the same, with the sole intention of killing you."

I closed my eyes and tried to remember any clue or signs I was being betrayed by either of them. It angered me to have to consider this. The girl in my dream warned me about the danger all around me, and yet I chose to believe the first thing I was told. Hoping for guidance, I closed my eyes. So much depended on every decision I made. It was vital I didn't get this one wrong.

I whispered quietly to myself, "Please help me once again, precious light."

My hands warmed and they were starting to glow again. The ice below Lucan and Simean's feet moved. A wall of ice formed around them. They banged on the wall to be released, but it was too thick for them to break it.

"I'm sorry, Lucan. I've been told repeatedly to trust my heart and instincts. I believe that Haygon's intentions are for good. However, my soul says you aren't to be trusted," I said to them.

Haygon removed his blindfold and placed his hand on my shoulder.

"Congratulations, Prince Eitan. I see you have the first key," Haygon said.

The intricate chrome was still warm in my hands as I lifted it to show them. It had two groves on the bottom and the top was woven with a tiny crown at the tip.

Lucan and Simean begged, "Please Prince Eitan! It is true, we were sent to find the keys and keep you from finding the armor. We would have never intentionally hurt you, though! You don't understand! Lord Kiverus will destroy us both if we don't-"

I interrupted, "Enough! You should be more concerned about what I could do to you for your betrayal, not Kiverus whom I have been preordained to destroy! You are no longer my companions nor do I care if you spend the rest of eternity in this cave!"

Rogelio spoke. "Don't worry Prince, the dogs are hungry." He glared intently at the two, and said, "They will not be here for all of eternity! They will provide a good dinner for the dogs." Rogelio produced a precarious grin.

His smile then turned humble as he asked if he could join the final battle.

"I have been stuck in this cave for as long as I can remember. It would be an honor fight beside you. I can help you," he said as his tuxedo changed into a suit of armor, "and I am willing to serve with the greatest of cost upon myself. You are going to change the worlds and restore everything as it should be. Rogelio De La Cueva is gladly at your service," he said as he reverently bowed before me.

His sincerity was touching. Surely he realized that such a small creature had very little protection to offer, yet he did so willingly.

I nodded my head at him and granted him his desire. A glowing light appeared from across the room. It was a portal, and we knew it was time to find the next key.

"I still don't trust him," Tucker said as he motioned toward Haygon.

"But you trust me, don't you?" I asked.

"Of course I do," Tucker answered.

"Haygon is going with us. I trust him," I replied.

I held Tucker's arm and looked at them both, "See you on the other side of wherever this leads."

"I'll be right behind you, my lord," Haygon replied.

"Just don't let go, Ethan. I hate this part!" Tucker said as we jumped into another unknown.

Chapter 17

The Fountain of Eternity flowed with water darker than had ever been seen before. The temple that used to shine brightly was now covered in darkness. Ivy engulfed every part of every wall where it concealed the wicked creatures that lay below it. The place where joy and hope used to reside, transformed into a place of despair and sorrow.

Lord Kiverus sat impatiently on his throne of self-righteousness. Furious the child was so close within reach and still managed to slip away. He heard the prophecies the same as everyone else, but he determined to prove them wrong. He should have been given the throne, and he wasn't about to let a child stand between him and his revenge. From the time before he was born, it seemed as if he was set apart and condemned. The Kruathans designed the worlds for their precious creations to reside in, yet his own brother banished from his home. How dare the Kruathans unjustly lay out this wicked path before him? So many times his requests to them were ignored. His pleas blatantly dismissed without reason. The Kruathans placed the Lathiaens in charge of maintaining Xaerdonia. He was a Lathiaen, yet his own family rejected him. He was banished from Xaerdonia unjustly, and the time neared when he would punish all who rejected him. He would obtain vengeance by destroying the very things the Kruathans worked so hard in creating. He was determined to prove his power to all the worlds, and to all of creation. He'd prove to the Kruathans he didn't need them, and although they refused to give him powers, he gained them on his own. It enraged him further to think about these things, the unjustness of it all.

His thoughts were interrupted by a disciple.

"Lord Kiverus, please forgive me for bringing disturbing news," he said with a lowered head and nervous bow.

Then he continued, "I've just learned Lucan and his men were unsuccessful. Eitan figured out Lucan was sent to kill him. It's madness. It's as if nature and all of its creatures heed to his command. He made it to The White Forest, and *through* it. Even Timordis had him within reach, but didn't stop him."

Lord Kiverus stood to his feet and the rage consumed him. He let out loud screams of frustration.

"There's more, my Lord," the disciple said.

Lord Kiverus turned with anticipated anger toward the disciple.

"He also found the first key. He took it and traveled to another world. We also discovered Haygon is with him," the disciple said quietly.

"*HAYGON?* Why has this disciple of mine not already destroyed this boy?" Lord Kiverus asked.

The disciple fearfully answered, "Once again, forgive me, my lord, but it appears he is actually helping him."

"Helping him! Where is this sabotage coming from? I will kill him too, I will kill them all!" Lord Kiverus exclaimed. "Be gone from my sight! I will take care of this detestable child myself!"

"But my lord-"

"I said leave!" Kiverus yelled.

The disciple left and Kiverus stood devoured in madness. He stormed out of the temple determined to destroy the great willow tree. It was the tree chosen to represent Xaerdonia and the tree the Kruathans used for communication. They refused to acknowledge him anytime he was ever in its presence, so it might as well be demolished. He saw no use for the tree any longer, and his objective was very clear.

He remembered the distinct path he traveled as a child. He followed the flow of water from the fountain in temple, through the garden, and into the large circle of trees. The willow tree rested in the center. Each tree represented a different world. He remembered when his father was the king how clean and pure the water appeared. The trees were so healthy and strong. Kiverus, vindictively satisfied, noticed the currently rotting condition of the trees. It was a visual reminder he was in control. It pleased him to know he poisoned the water in such a way it was slowly killing the worlds. He probably could've destroyed them by now, but it was much more gratifying to watch them slowly suffer.

He first passed by the apple tree. The fruit that was once as large as his hands had now shriveled to the size of tiny rocks. The trees made an uneasy sound as they sensed his presence.

The mighty oak tree, that once stood tall and proud, now drooped with weakness. The trees blew harder, and Kiverus heard a voice being carried with the wind. His attention was drawn to the cypress tree. It was unusual that while all the other trees continued to rot and decay, the cypress tree continued to grow stronger. It was the very reason his attention was consumed with it. It was the one tree he was forbidden to approach as a child.

"Kiverus. Come closer," a voice said.

He heard the voice coming from near the cypress tree.

"Who dares speak my name?" he responded. "Reveal yourself!"

A small black scorpion crawled to the top of the tree roots.

"I can help you," hissed the scorpion.

"Help me? I don't need your help! Don't you know who I am, you stupid creature?" Kiverus argued.

"But I *can* help. I have powers that would greatly benefit you," the scorpion replied.

Kiverus's interest was captivated with the thoughts of more power.

"What kind of power? Who are you?" he asked.

The scorpion let out a nasty hiss and continued, "We are already connected. The powers you have came from me. I'm cursed to this vulgar existence by the same ones you seek revenge against. I can help you."

"You are the one, aren't you?" Kiverus asked. "You are the one that stung my mother when she was pregnant with me. You are the reason I have suffered and been ridiculed. You are the one that changed everything!"

Kiverus raised his hand and a dark light projected from it. "You will die for what you've done to me!"

He released his power directly onto the scorpion. He expected the scorpion to completely disintegrated, yet it remained untouched.

"You cannot destroy me!" the scorpion hissed. "I've been cursed and damned to this tree for all of eternity. I have not always been in this form. In fact, at one time I appeared more like you. Your desire is to kill Prince Eitan and gain the Sacred Armor. I can help you."

"How can *you* help *me*?" asked Kiverus.

The voice hissed in return, "I can tell you where the boy is. I can provide bloodthirsty beasts that will find him and destroy him. I can make you stronger and together we will challenge the Kruathans and rule together for all of eternity."

Kiverus pondered the words.

"And what do you want in return? If you had this power all along, why have you waited until now to use it?" he asked.

"I have tried once before, but I was unable to completely inject myself," the scorpion answered.

"You mean my mother. You tried to inject yourself into her?" Kiverus replied.

The scorpion's hisses became louder and echoed through the air.

"No! I had no interest in her. I wanted you! Your father stopped me before I finished. My venom has grown stronger with you through the years. It gave you the power to do things you wouldn't have been able to do without it. Time has always been on my side. I have waited patiently for you to grow, for your powers to grow. You *must* see I am already a part of you. I am so much a part of you that you would die without me. Now it is time to allow the rest of me to join you."

Kiverus walked closer to the scorpion as it continued, "You are a powerful ruler. Together we can be unstoppable. The Kruathans could have prevented all of this if they had chosen to do so. Yet, they chose to let you suffer. Let us finish this!"

Kiverus warily considered what the scorpion said. He always sensed a greater power inside of himself, and also sensed he was missing a part of his soul. He hated the Kruathans with such great intensity, but this was not a time for misplaced trust.

The scorpion sensed his hesitation.

"You are the most powerful being in *most* of the worlds. Yet, there are some that still hold more power than you, the Kruathans. I know how to reach them. I know their weaknesses. I know how to make them bow to your authority. This is so much more than a simple child who is trying to destroy you. This is about having the greatest authority in ALL of the worlds. It is about being the utmost authority and ruler, even over the Kruathans. It is the only way to make them pay for what they have done to us!"

"How do I know it will be as you say?" Kiverus asked as he considered the offer. "How can I be assured you aren't just trying to deceive me as well?"

The scorpion raised its tail and a black mist surrounded him. Kiverus was paralyzed and his hand was forced out as the scorpion climbed his arm leaving a trail of black shadows wherever he crawled. He stopped when he reached Kiverus's neck. Kiverus heard the whispering chants and hissing directly behind his ear. Instantly, the scorpion stabbed Kiverus's neck and injected not only his venom, but his entire being into Kiverus's body. The empty shell of the scorpion fell to the ground below. Kiverus felt the instantaneous power surge and felt stronger than ever. He felt another soul sharing his body, and was satisfied with the power the new creature brought with him. Their souls began to intertwine as if they were instantly becoming one.

His hands lifted into the air as he chanted, "Ades malas bestias inferni! Tempus perdere!"

Wailing and howling filled the air. He summoned forth three beasts. They were hideous with gnashing fangs. Truly unique in design, the scaly solid white creatures walked on all fours. Their eyes naturally a bright blue, but once in Kiverus's presence, their eyes became the same hollow and empty gray color he had. He bent down closer to them as they approached him. The beasts were covered with the foul odor of death, and their slobber was tinged with blood.

Kiverus spoke quietly at first, "You know why you are here, don't you?"

"Yes," the beasts breathed.

"I need you to find him. I need you to destroy him. I no longer want him brought back alive. I want him ripped into shreds from the surface of his skin to the depths of his soul and his remains spread throughout all the worlds. Do you understand?"

"Yes," the beasts replied.

"Go! Destroy him!" Kiverus demanded as the beasts fled.

Raeden couldn't help but feel responsible as he sat in his limited cell. His cell was directly across from Thalesten and Giana's.

"Keep your faith, my king and queen. Eitan is strong. The Kruathans will help him. He'll make it here. I know he will," said Raeden.

"I'm not sure how much longer I can be strong," Giana said quietly. "I've waited so long. It's hard to imagine the child I once held so close, is no longer a child. I wish I could have had more time with him. I've missed him so dearly."

Thalesten took her hand through the bars and held it.

"It has been a long time, love, but the wait is almost over. He has been predestined for great things, things that will change the worlds forever," Thalesten said.

"I can't stand being held captive like this! I should be out there helping him, protecting him!" Raeden said, frustrated.

"Don't do this, Raeden. You saved his life. You placed him in a safe and loving home, and kept a close watch on him for years. When Kiverus's disciples got close, you led them astray for several more years. We couldn't have asked for more. I couldn't have asked for more!" said Giana.

Thalesten chuckled a little to himself. "I wonder what your father thought of him?"

Giana's curiosity raised, "What do you mean?"

"Well, I'm sure he's made it to the Candraen haven by now. I'd love to have seen the look on Caedmius' face when he saw his only grandson for the first time," Thalesten replied.

"I didn't think about that!" Giana said. "It *is* the first time he's ever seen Eitan! He was on his way to visit us on that horrible day when everything changed, and he never got to see him."

"He resembles you greatly, my lady," Raeden said. "There were so many times I saw visions of you through his eyes when he was younger."

"I wish your father would've learned to trust Haygon. When Haygon visited a few months ago, he said the stubborn old man was still suspicious after all these years," Thalesten said to Giana.

"He doesn't even believe we are alive. Maybe he will believe Haygon's words after he's seen Eitan. Haygon has been a wonderful help to both nations, even if they don't realize it," Giana replied.

"I'm sure this sparked a new fire in the conspiracy between the two nations. By now, they've both heard the news of Prince Eitan's return. There's no telling what rumors started about your existence," Raeden said.

"The truth will be revealed soon enough. Soon both nations will know the truth and they will be united. Together, and led by Eitan, they will defeat Kiverus. Then, all things will be pure once again. Our family will be rightfully restored to the throne, and all balance will be restored to all the worlds," Thalesten said.

Noise came from within the hallway. It was the guards.

A woman screamed, "Please! No! Leave him alone!"

There was a struggle as they dragged a young man from his cell.

"Someone help! Please! They are taking my son! Help him!" she screamed with terror.

"I love you, Mother! Be strong! It won't be much longer!"

His voice faded as he was forced violently down the long hallway. The iron door slammed behind them as they left. The only sound remaining was of a mother's cries.

"I can't do this much longer, Thalesten," said Giana with a whisper.

"Haygon says when Kiverus sacrifices the Candraens he gains power from them. They believe he's hoping to gain enough power so he'll have the ability to travel. He's become very strong and powerful by stealing their abilities. He believes he'll be able to challenge the Kruathans if he can find their world," Thalesten said.

"That's impossible," Giana said with disgust.

"It seems impossible, but only because no one has ever tried. He believes he's stronger than they are. He believes he'll take over and seat his throne in place of theirs," replied Raeden.

Thalesten interrupted, "The Kruathans are more powerful than any force or any creation that has ever existed! You should not allow your thoughts to consider anything otherwise. They do not have to fight Kiverus in order to prove their greatness."

"He'll make a wonderful King to Xaerdonia," Giana said.

"First, he needs to make it here. And let us hope that it is a speedy voyage home," Thalesten said with a slight smile.

Chapter 18

I wasn't sure how much further we could travel without regaining some energy and strength. I was exhausted, and I knew Tucker and Haygon were also. We stood in amazement at the new place we were brought. We were completely surrounded by sand as far as we could see. Almost instantly, we shed our heavy coats that kept us warm in the last world. There weren't any trees, which meant no shade. I had no idea of which direction we should travel, nor did I have any guidance from the sky. I looked for the sun in hopes of determining the east from the west, but the sun wasn't there. It was certainly another strange place.

"How is it so hot if there isn't even a sun in the sky?" I asked without a reply. I suppose I didn't really expect an answer. The sweat began to trickle down Tucker's face.

"We need to take a break," I suggested.

"Here? In the heat?" Tucker asked.

"He's right. We have no idea how far we may have to travel before finding shade," Haygon responded.

I bent down and reached into my backpack. I remembered the sack that Aletheya gave me and wondered what might be inside of it. There were three pieces of fruit inside. I handed one to Tucker and one to Haygon.

"I've never seen fruit like this before," I said while examining it.

"I have," said Tucker. "Abigeal gave me some. This is the fruit I was telling you about, Ethan. You know, the fruit and tea that made me see clearly. It's delicious," Tucker said as he took a large bite.

I took a bite of the fruit and was quite surprised myself. It most certainly *was* one of the best tasting foods I'd ever had. I bet my mother could've made some amazing deserts with this. My mother. My thoughts raced back to reality. It was still hard to grasp the fact the woman I'd always called mother, wasn't my natural mother. I had a whole other family I knew nothing about.

"You said you know my parents well?" I asked Haygon.

"Yes, your majesty. Your father and I grew up together. Your grandfather and my father were best friends. I suppose it's only right their children walk in the same footsteps and continue the friendship," Haygon said.

"Do you have any children?" I asked Haygon.

"No," Haygon responded with a distant look.

"Didn't you ever want to have children?" I asked him.

"It wasn't written in my destiny to have children," he said.

His look turned from distant to content as he spoke, "I am fully satisfied with the path laid before me. It's been the highest honor to serve your grandfather, your father, and now you. I regret nothing." Haygon spoke with great sincerity.

It was unbelievable how filling and rejuvenating this one piece of fruit was. The temperature didn't seem quite so hot now, and Tucker looked very comfortable as he stretched his legs above the bed of sand. The reality of the whole situation became frightening and like a tremendous weight.

"What if I'm not strong enough?" I asked quietly.

"My lord? What do you mean?" Haygon replied.

"I just mean, what if I fail? What if I can't do what everyone, and everything, is depending on me to do?"

Confirming my doubt, a foreboding chill brushed against my spine.

"I think I feel him," I said with an uneasy tone.

"Feel whom? Lord Kiverus?" Haygon anxiously asked.

"Yeah. Is that possible? He's my uncle and we share the same blood. It's strange I know, but it's as if I can feel his power growing. Something has changed. I think he knows where we are. I'm not sure I'm ready for this," I said reluctantly.

"My dear prince, you may not understand it fully yet, but it is your weaknesses that will make you strong. There is no such book, or knowledge known, that will accurately describe the qualities of a mighty hero. Look," he said as he pulled the book from my backpack.

He opened it to the beginning and I saw the pictures of Xaerdonia. I saw pictures of my grandfather, my parents, and even my birth. He continued to flip through the pages. I saw pictures of Tucker and I back at the Candraen haven. Tucker sat up to get a closer look for himself.

"Those pages weren't in there before," I said.

Haygon smiled as he continued to turn the pages. I became sick to my stomach reliving the horrific events involving the Timordis. The pages showed Aletheya giving me the first key. I sat in awe when he flipped to the last page and I saw the four of us just as we were. The drawing showed us sitting in a desert looking at the book.

"You see, my prince, your story isn't complete yet. Although you have a path laid before you, and you are told your destiny, it is only *you* that can write the pages of your life. It is certain you will make mistakes. It is what you learn from your mistakes and shortcomings that matters most.

"Some would choose to stand and mock the strong man as he stumbles and falls. Some would choose to keep count of a man's failures and tell him how he should have done better. There is no honor or integrity that comes from that behavior." Haygon surveyed my attentiveness as he continued. "The honor is given to the man that hears the voice of hopelessness and despair roaring in his ears, invading into the depths of his thoughts, and assaulting his very soul, yet he remains firm in the battle. Although he is bruised, beaten, and exhausted, he remains strong because he is driven by his courage, his faith, his love, and his greatness. He will refuse to give in to defeat, and surrendering is not an option." He leaned in as if he was going to reveal a secret and spoke softer. "Even yet, he is wise beyond measure because he has learned the very core of his strength was created by his mistakes and failures. He knows had it not been for the battles, there would not have been ambition and purpose. Without ambition and purpose, the voice of defeat would triumph. What you must come to realize is regardless of whether or not you *feel* strong enough, the battle is indeed approaching quickly. The most difficult tasks still remain. Your thoughts and determination are under attack and you must not give in to their deceitful words."

I knew he was giving valuable advice. "You have been given guidance and leading only you can understand. You have a wonderful gift inside you that you have yet to fully discover. You must patiently endure the remainder of your journey and trials in order to discover the depths of your nobility and greatness. You and you alone, were chosen for this magnificent calling. Remain truly steadfast with your heart, soul, and mind, and you will overcome everything you encounter."

My burdens were lifting. I knew he was right. I knew I could overcome any circumstance and conquer any tyrant. I felt the victory running through my blood. The courage inside of me swelled to the point I felt the ground shaking. It was at that very moment I realized the ground really *was* shaking, and it wasn't me doing it.

We all jumped to our feet in anticipation of what was happening. The sand blew and shifted beneath our feet. It rose in front of me and its force knocked me back down. Swirling in thousands of tiny circles, the sand formed the shape of a small man, and then everything was still once again. The curiosity and uncertainty was apparent.

"What is it?" asked Tucker.

I looked to Haygon for answers, but he offered none. My hand shook as I reached out to touch it.

"Hello!" shouted the sand figure as his eyes popped open.

He took his hands and brushed them along his body as if he was trying to sweep off the sand off his clothes. He was very unusual indeed. He was short and had all the features of a middle aged man, even some wrinkles. Every part of him was made from the sand and was all tan colored except his eyes. His eyes had colors of white and blue, but were curiously still made of sand.

"My name is Harent," he said as he turned to evaluate the company he was with. "I have been sent to locate the Prince and guide him in the direction of Monscretus where he will discover the armor he searches for."

His assessment ceased when he turned his attention toward me.

"Ah! You must be the one!" he exclaimed as he quickly bowed before me. "Welcome Prince Eitan. Come, follow me. I must first take you to my kingdom where you will meet my princess. She's waited for your arrival many years now."

Everything happened so quickly we hadn't even noticed the fruit had returned our energy and health to its utmost condition. Tucker walked closely to Harent as he inspected the strange little man. I followed slightly further back with Haygon. I knew there was more to his greatness than what he had mentioned and I had an intense desire to learn more about him.

"I don't mean for this to sound rude, but was your family like servants to mine or something?" I asked Haygon.

He raised an eyebrow as he looked at me, and then he chuckled a little.

"Not quite, my Prince. I guess you could say that we were more like advisors," he answered. His remaining smile indicated that he wasn't offended by my asking.

"Like I said before, it has always been a joy serving your father and grandfather. They are extraordinary leaders and are fully deserving of their noble duties," Haygon said.

"So you also grew up with Kiverus?" I asked.

"Yes. Kiverus was always there. Although it seemed he preferred to play in the shadows instead of the sun. Thalesten and I often saw Kiverus secretly sneaking around to observe what we were doing. There were many times Thalesten asked him to join us, but he consistently refused. There was a time even I hoped he would change and open his heart, but that day never came. Things changed drastically when Armon, your grandfather, and the Candraen king arranged a marriage for their children. This was done in hopes the two nations would unite through Thalesten and Giana's child, you. However, this only further enraged Kiverus. The Kruathans had a plan though, they've always had a plan," Haygon said with a solemn smile.

"So why did you portray yourself as a disciple of Kiverus? Isn't that betraying my parents?" I asked.

Haygon answered, "It was actually your father's idea. When Armon announced the engagement and his plans for bringing the nations together, Thalesten knew Kiverus's rage would reach new heights. I distanced myself from Thalesten and your family. I did so thinking that Kiverus would be fooled when I pledged myself to him. It has been very hard to contain all of these secrets. Neither Armon nor the Candraen King knew of our intentions. It was years before I saw Thalesten again. When Lord Kiverus imprisoned Thalesten and Giana, it was much easier to communicate with them since there were no suspicions with the disciples going to the prison. Your location was unknown for nearly fifteen years. Your parents have waited in anticipation for your return home."

Tucker was still amazed over the little man made of sand.

"Excuse me for staring, I've just never seen anything like this before," Tucker said to Harent.

"Quite all right, sir. I did plenty of my own staring when this curse first came to be on my kingdom," Harent replied.

"You mean you haven't always been this way?" asked Tucker.

"No sir, not always this way," replied Harent. "We too have been waiting a long time for our kingdom to be restored. Your Prince is the answer to the curse's undoing."

"When you first appeared, you looked at each one of us. How did you know he was the prince?" Tucker hesitated, "I mean, why him? Why didn't you assume it was me?"

Harent smiled as he explained, "You see sir, we were told the prince would have an unmistakable light inside of him. It is a gift that the Kruathans gave him. It is a light people in your world probably do not recognize yet."

Tucker's expression changed as Harent spoke.

"Your world isn't as you remember it right now. Lord Kiverus created such a destruction it has temporarily suspended time in your world."

"I know. I heard that before when we were at the Candraen haven. It doesn't make sense to me though," Tucker replied.

"All of creation is depending on your friend. He has been chosen and has the power to set things back how they once were, if he so chooses. If he fails and isn't successful, all worlds are destined to be slowly destroyed by the wickedness inside of Lord Kiverus," Harent explained.

"You see friend, the Kruathans will not allow the sands of time to remain still forever. They have chosen this young prince for a reason, and they have given him a very special gift only they could give. He is destined for greatness. I suspect they have a greater plan and fate than we could ever imagine."

Harent looked at the sky as if he were searching for something, and then he continued. "There is so much more I am sure we are unaware of. I am guessing if this young prince is successful, he will soon be presented with an even greater adventure."

Everything seemed so strange to Tucker. He never limited himself to completely dismiss the thought of other worlds, but he honestly never imagined the events and things he recently witnessed.

We came to a stop. Standing before us was a large wall of sand. It went as far as I could see in both directions. Harent informed us it was the once mighty wall that surrounded his kingdom. The sand on the wall began to trickle like a giant waterfall. It revealed a face well over twenty feet tall. We took a few steps back in order to gain a full view of this magnificent creation. The image was a tree with winding roots that now covered the bottom of the great wall.

"Hello, you stubborn giant tree!" Harent yelled toward the wall. "It's me again, it's Harent! Let us in!"

The tree slowly opened its eyes as more sand flowed downward. Large branches extended out as arms and shook violently as they stretched. Sand filled the air as the face in the wall casually yawned.

"All right already! We need in! I am escorting the Prince to meet Princess Caetrin!" Harent exclaimed with more frustration.

A great burst of laughter came from the tree and startled all of us.

"Da prince, eh? Ya want me to think ya found da prince? I suppose ya referrin' to da prince dat gonna fix dis fallen kingdom?"

The tree chuckled with such force the ground felt unstable beneath our feet. Harent's body fell apart as shaken sand and then resumed its form again.

The tree reached toward Harent and poked at him while speaking,

"Ah Harent, ya always be da funny one. Ya know I like givin' ya a hard time."

"You stupid, ignorant wall! I'm not trying to be funny. I am being very serious!" he insisted.

Harent grabbed me and pushed me close to the wall.

"Look at him! Can't you see it?" Harent demanded of the tree.

The laughter stilled. The tree's eyes blinked several times before its mouth gasped open in awe.

"I see it, Harent. I be darned, ya *did* find da prince!" the tree exclaimed with great enthusiasm.

"Thank you. Now will you please let us enter?" Harent asked.

The tree spoke with a more serious tone, saying, "Of course I will let ya enter. Ya been gone for a while dis time, Harent. Things change a little more since ya been gone. Be careful, da kingdom is sinkin' and gettin' harder to find."

The sand that formed the tree's mouth began to shift until it was fully opened.

Harent pointed as he said, "This way," and walked into the tree's mouth.

I'd seen pictures of sand castles and other spectacular images that were created with sand, but I'd never seen anything like this. It was an entire kingdom made of sand. The castle and other buildings looked as if they were trampled in a war. The castle towers were lying on the ground along with parts of the outer wall.

"It used to be quite stunning before it fell," Harent said as he motioned toward the fallen castle. "This is my kingdom. That used to be my home. I was a servant of the great king for many years, many wonderful years," he continued.

I touched part of a castle stone as we walked by. It was amazing the sand formed in such a way it was still very strong and sturdy. I imagined it must have been a great force that caused all of this damage. I began to ask what happened to the kingdom when another person appeared from the sand. This time, it was a woman. She was considerably beautiful despite the matter from which she formed. Her crown glistened in the light.

Harent bowed before her as he spoke,

"Princess Caetrin, I have found Prince Eitan and have brought him to you."

Her voice was very soft and pure.

"Well done, Harent. Thank you for your service. My father would be very proud," she said.

We followed her to the inner courtyard and took seats on large logs made of sand.

"Princess, what has happened to your kingdom? Why is it this way?" I questioned.

She reached her hand into her pocket and returned with more of the delicious fruit we had eaten earlier.

"Here. Take some and put it in your bag for later, you may get hungry," she offered.

I felt a gentle peck on my shoulder. I turned to find a very confused friend as he whispered to me, "What are we supposed to do with fruit made of sand?"

I shrugged my shoulders and reached to take the fruit. As it was placed into my hand, it changed from the rough sand to soft fleshy fruit. The princess giggled at the shocked looks upon our faces.

"Many things change, Prince Eitan. Things do not ever remain the same. Our kingdom was once great and mighty, it also changed. I was only a child myself when it happened. One day my brother, the prince, was out exploring the land as small children do. A mysterious scorpion caught his curious attention. He captured the scorpion and brought it back to our father, the king, because it was so unusual. We have always had sand scorpions, but this one was strange and uncommon to any that we had ever seen before.

The King consulted his council and they determined it was wicked and should be burned. They set fire to the small jar in which it was contained. As soon as the fire touched it, it instantly turned to sand. It was shortly after, a terrible storm came, and sands from the depths of the ocean poured onto the village with rage and vengeance. All of our castles and homes were turned to sand, including our people. We were forever cursed to remain this way until the chosen one could come and restore balance to Xaerdonia. You *are* our only hope, Prince Eitan."

"I've come to realize that," I said. "I am searching for two more keys that will allow me to acquire the Sacred Armor."

"Yes, it is crucial you find what you are looking for. Lord Kiverus must be destroyed. I wish for you to return one day to our kingdom, when it has been restored. I wish for you to celebrate with us when time isn't so critical."

She turned to Harent and spoke with urgency.

"Harent, you must take Prince Eitan to the far end of the kingdom and direct him towards Monscretus, where he will find the final key."

Harent nodded in agreement.

"Forgive me, Princess Caetrin, but I don't even have the second key yet," I said.

She embraced me and kissed me on the cheek. Her hand reached once again into her pocket returning this time with the key.

"Please promise me you will succeed, you will not give up, and you will be strong until the end. Promise me you will restore our kingdom when you take back your righteous throne," she pleaded.

"I promise," I said. I was determined to finish.

She spoke with assured faith. "My people were told hundreds of years ago to protect this key. We were told a time would come when a great warrior would come searching for it. We would know when the time was right, and it would be the key to restoring our kingdom. I give it to you with great hope in my heart."

She held out the key. Just like the fruit, when I touched the key it turned from sand to its original form. She sighed deeply, handed me a tiny pouch, and told me to open it as she poured sand into it. She said I would know what to do with it when the time was right. Her words wished us well as we followed Harent out of the castle and toward the edge of the kingdom.

Chapter 19

Standing there on the edge of the kingdom, the rest of the world appeared to be in view. Surprisingly, there wasn't sand everywhere. The sand began and ended within the kingdom's boundaries. Surveying the route leading to Monscretus was slightly distressing.

Harent pointed to a dark and shadowy valley below us.

"It is known as The Valley of Unknown Shadows and Darkness," he said with admonition.

I felt the darkness ascending to the place we stood and Harent took a firm grasp on my arm. It startled me and I saw even more intense fear within his eyes. The ground tremored and we all took a few steps away from the edge.

"The wicked has found you, Prince Eitan!" Harent spoke hastily and with tremendous fear.

Tucker's face was overcome with astonishment as he spoke, "Ethan, look! The castle, it's sinking!"

"Prince Eitan, you must find solid ground quickly!" Harent demanded as his legs were shaken to nothing. His hand began to lose its solidness as he pointed to the tremendous mountain that eclipsed the horizon.

"You must reach the top of Monscretus!" Harent exclaimed.

"The top of the mountain is Monscretus?" Tucker frantically demanded. "How do you suppose we are to reach the top? Sorry, but I forgot to pack my climbing gear!"

As the ground began to quake and throb uncontrollably, the mountain became the least of my concerns. Haygon began sinking in the sand as if it were quicksand.

"Help him!" I demanded of everyone around me. Harent was almost completely gone when he begged me to find solid ground before it was too late, and Haygon struggled harder to free himself. I instinctively made my way over to him.

The ground was too unstable and I felt Tucker's hand on my shoulder.

"Ethan! We need to find solid ground! How?" he asked with words filled with sternness.

Haygon quit struggling against the collapsing ground and his face filled with content.

"I have finished the task set before me. Now it is your turn to finish an even greater task," he said.

I screamed as I realized he was complacent with the fate he was about to receive. My foot stumbled on something extremely hard as I tried to maneuver closer to him. As the sand disappeared further, it became apparent the hard thing was a solid rock. Tucker, also sinking, was only able to grab my ankle. I reached back and helped him onto the rock with me. I quickly lunged forward to reach out for Haygon, only to realize he was no longer there. It felt as though my heart had been ripped out and tossed into the sinking sand along with him. I was so overtaken by determination I was disregarding the boundary limitations of the rock. Tucker grabbed both of my shoulders and forced me to the ground.

"Stop, Ethan! He's gone! If you die with him, so does everything else!" he reasoned.

I sat there on the rock staring into the unknown of the world for quite some time before speaking.

"Ethan. Are you ok? We really need to figure out a way off of this thing and get moving," Tucker suggested.

"I failed him," I muttered.

"What? Ethan, you heard him. You heard his last words just as I did. He knew it was his time, and he was ok with it. His dying wish was for you to finish what was started," Tucker replied.

Tucker moved and sat down beside me.

"Ethan, there are so many people that still need you to finish this." He laughed quietly, "Man, I'd love to have some of your mom's homemade cooking right now."

There was complete sincerity on his face when he spoke.

"I miss home. I miss my parents. I even miss some of the things I hated so much before," he said.

I closed my eyes and would've given just about anything if I could get one more hug from my mom. I knew she wasn't my birth mother, but she'd always be the woman I call mother. I thought about Kallie and how beautiful she looked the night at Dane's party. Just when everything seemed like it was getting better, everything had to change. Even if I *am* successful in defeating Kiverus, would my world ever be the same? I personally had changed a lot.

As a tear fell from my eye, it landed on the necklace the lady from my dream gave me. It began to glow as bright as a star in the sky. Tucker smiled and I knew I wasn't given the option to fail. Failure was not in my destiny! I stood to my feet and looked around for a way off the giant rock. The dark and shadowy valley was still beneath us. As much as neither of us wanted to have to go through it, we knew it was the only way to reach Monscretus. I wondered if Liora was still with me. Even though I knew she *wasn't* Kallie, I still enjoyed seeing and hearing her. I closed my eyes and concentrated on her, hoping she would return. It was easy to focus on her considering how much she resembled Kallie. I was so focused I could smell her as if she were standing right behind me. I was frustrated when she didn't answer.

Then, I heard a voice whisper. I assumed it was Tucker.

"Look, over here," it said.

I opened my eyes and the rock's edge was gaping where Tucker stood.

"Amazing, Tucker! Why didn't we see this before?" I asked.

"See what?" he asked confused.

"The stairs. Where did they come from?" I replied.

Tucker looked down in amazement and stated he had no idea. *"Liora?"* I thought to myself. I could have sworn it was

Tucker's voice I heard. The stairs wrapped in a coil leading down the entire rock. It was a long and exhausting journey down. As we neared the bottom, the entrance into the valley appeared before us. The bright sky that had been apparent all day was now overshadowed. Fear and uncertainty protruded from the valley and attempted to sway our spirits. The sound of the wild penetrated every thought of serenity and calmness. The very air we breathed seemed as though it was poisoned with a vile motive.

"It's strange isn't it?" Tucker asked.

"What's that?" I replied.

"You can feel it," Tucker paused as he focused on a particular tree branch. "I didn't even realize it was something that could be seen. But not only do I *see* the darkness, I *feel* it," he continued.

The branch Tucker watched had an unusual rhythm to its movement. It wasn't apparent at first glance, but it held something that made it move in such a unique manner. Motionless, ghostly eyes stared back at us. Sallow shades of yellow and amber examined us as if we were prey. They belonged to the largest crow I had ever seen in my life. Suddenly, the crow thrust himself forward while releasing a blood curling "Ca Caaaaw," that suggested an unpromising warning.

He flew above the trees creating intense calamity amongst the other fowl as they left their own perches to engage in the chaos. The trees themselves seemed to participate by whispering sinister winds to each other.

Our only option was to follow the pathway into the darkness and hope we could withstand whatever the swampy forest encompassed. If for nothing else, I was thankful there was a clear path for us. We were becoming drained once again, and I certainly didn't feel like creating one.

Minutes turned to hours the further we walked, and the atmosphere brought us down with each step. A thin fog developed which made things more difficult and Tucker managed to trip over every stick or rock on the ground. He made me incredibly nervous. It was hard enough to see for myself without trying to see for the both of us. I knew we were getting closer to water when my feet got harder to lift out of the muck and mud. We arrived at a small clearing and the swampy water was clear in sight.

"I'm *not* going through that water!" Tucker said without hesitation.

I looked around to see if there was another way to reach the bank on the other side.

"*Seriously*. I'm *not* going through that water!" Tucker insisted once again.

I noticed a small wooden bridge camouflaged by the darkness of the trees.

"There," I said as I pointed to it.

Obviously, it wasn't a logical solution to getting across, but it was the only solution we had. It held together by old, worn ropes and some of the boards were missing. Other boards were so low to the water we might as well have just waded in the water.

"Come on Tuck, it's the best option we have," I said.

I wanted to reassure him, but I couldn't even convince myself.

"I'll go first," I said as I tugged on the ropes to examine their strength.

Tucker looked as though he was going to have an anxiety attack. I placed my foot on the first board and it broke immediately into the murky water. Trying to balance the ropes, I stretched my leg out to the second board. It was much more stable.

"Just follow in my footsteps," I said, with more confidence this time.

It was a challenge trying to stretch far enough to step over the questionable looking boards. I hesitated to turn around and see if Tucker was still standing on the bank or if he was going to follow. I knew the answer when the ropes began to shake uncontrollably that he'd chosen to follow. I was about halfway across the bridge before I felt comfortable enough to glance at the water below. It was disgusting. It looked more like a giant oil spill than water of any kind.

There was movement lurking beneath the surface. The sounds that previously filled the air had become exceptionally quiet adding to the suspense. The water below us became less dense and flowed more freely, yet it was still morbidly dark. I kept moving forward as I realized it wasn't a time to sightsee, and the movement continued just beneath the surface. It was if something was following us, or maybe leading us. I wasn't sure, but I was certain it was distracting me. The water changed from a lucid gray color to a glowing white as the movement also increased.

"Ethan! What's all that motion in the water up there? Should I be concerned?" Tucker asked.

He spoke with apprehension, " It's too far to turn back now!"

"I don't know what it is, but I think we're all right. If it wanted to harm us, it would've done so already," I said trying to reason.

The water formed a sparkling clear circle around the area with the movement. I leaned slightly over the rope to see a beautiful Koi fish serenely swimming in the water. It was so white it was almost glowing. The dark oily water was separated from the water the fish swam in. Everywhere the fish swam, the water would momentarily become translucent. I wondered if there were any more in the water, but it was the only one I saw. Tucker, finally catching up to me, added weight on the bridge causing boards to break and fall. The ropes ahead of us were weakening also. Without further warning, the entire bridge collapsed plunging us both into the water. The light from the Koi surrounded us and we were actually able to see the bottom of the swamp. The remarkable fish swam in between us and we were able to make it safely to the other bank.

We watched as the only light we saw faded back into the depths of the water. I followed the water upstream, and Tucker trailed slightly behind me. The sky above us began to have more light to it. We followed the water until it ran straight into some boulders. A small tunnel was formed in one of the rocks and we followed through it. A magnificent waterfall was in front of us. The water, black as night, flowed freely from the rocks of the waterfall. Of course we'd never seen a black waterfall before and were both quite intrigued by its beauty and uniqueness.

I approached the edge of the water and glanced into it only to find my reflection. There was exhaustion in my eyes. Tucker scooped some up in his hands and made a comment about wishing it was drinking water. As dark as it was around us, it was very tranquil listening to the sound of the falling water.

As I looked at my reflection, I saw a change in myself, yet I felt the same. My eyes began to ripple in the water and I knew something was about to happen. They instantly turned into the haunting gray I learned to hate so much. I knew the eyes belonged to Kiverus. Terrified of the unknown, Tucker and I preceded to move quickly out of the black lagoon we'd entered. Our pace quickened almost as much as our heartbeats.

I thought Tucker was crazy at first when he mentioned the tree limbs looked like arms and hands. The faster we tried to reach the mountain, the more I realized he was right. The birds and other creatures of the forest had resumed their noise making, and the sounds were so loud it made it hard to concentrate. Our pace turned to a quickened jog. It felt as though someone, or something, was following us. No. More like hunting us.

"Ethan! I can't look back, but I feel it chasing us," Tucker said between breaths.

"I know, Tuck. I feel it too," I said confirming his thoughts.

I noticed something in the distance and made my way towards it.

"Tuck, this way!" I said.

There was an ancient altar. The columns were only half standing where they once formed a circle. We stood in the middle with our backs together. It was instinct realizing we needed to be able to see all around us. As we attempted to catch our breath, the chaotic noise had seized yet again. It was suddenly and completely silent.

"It's awful quiet," Tucker whispered.

"Yeah," was about all I could mutter.

We both intently listened for any sound.

"I hear water again," I said.

"I don't hear anything," Tucker replied.

At this point it entered my mind that I could have been hallucinating, but I also heard faint singing.

"You don't hear that?" I asked.

"No. Nothing man," Tucker quickly replied.

The anxiety left my body. I was drawn to the sounds I heard.

"I hear it now," Tucker said.

It was a very distinct and alluring sound. Our thoughts clouded as we were pulled to it. We walked side by side as the singing continued beckoning to our spirits. There was another waterfall, but this one wasn't making any sound. Its color was most unusually black with stripes of white mixed in. It was quite odd. The singing continued, and we soon saw where it came from.

She stood close to the waterfall in a shallow area of the lagoon. All we saw was her back, but there was no doubt the hypnotizing song was coming from her. Everything about her was intriguing. She wore a long white gown that swayed gently in the water around her ankles. Her long dark hair looked like curls of silk as they brushed against her bare back. As if she was clueless to our presence, she gracefully bent down and ran her fingers across the surface of the water creating a slight ripple. I felt like we were invading her privacy, but I couldn't find the strength to turn away.

Two new voices joined the singing, and the two beautiful creatures that just appeared from the darkness walked toward her. Their hair was long and covered their bodies almost completely. In one quick glimpse, we noticed these two weren't wearing any clothing beneath their beautiful layers of hair. Their skin was so smooth and milky white without a single flaw anywhere.

Tucker whispered, "Are they bathing? Do you think they know we are here?"

I shrugged without an answer. The second girl whispered to the first, causing her to turn her head slowly over her shoulder towards me. It was the first time I was able to see any part of her face. All I saw were her eyes, but they seemed so familiar. They were the most enticing shade of green and her long lashes intensified her stare when they blinked.

"Dude. She's looking at you," Tucker said, sounding both excited and thrilled.

The other two girls made eye contact with Tucker as they began to bath each other. I could have sworn I heard his jaw hit the ground. They motioned for him to come to them.

"Uh. Dude. You know, we *haven't* showered in a few days. Why not do it in style?" he said as he began to unbutton his shirt.

Tucker took one step forward and I strained to keep my mind out of the trance it was trying so hard to enter. I grabbed his arm.

"Wait," I said.

The woman revealed her whole face to me now and I saw the reason for the familiarity. It was Kallie. Well, it appeared to be Kallie. Her tongue moved softly across her lips as she lifted her finger and motioned for me. Tucker was under a spell as he kept pulling forward and away from me.

"Wait, Tucker!" I said more firmly this time.

She didn't move her lips to talk, yet I heard her thoughts.

"*Come to me Prince Eitan. Let me give you what your heart desires,*" she said.

My heart anxiously beat faster. Something was wrong. Her words remained the same, but they started to sound deeper and more like hissing. I jerked Tucker's arm pretty hard and he stood still. There wasn't a noticeable moon, but the sky filled with an illuminating blue. There became enough light and my attention directed to the reflections in the water of the three women. Her reflection revealed the evil and wicked creature she really was.

I whispered hoping Tucker heard me.

"Look. Look in the water, man," I said quietly.

Tucker instantly snapped out of it and amazingly we knew what the other was thinking, "Run!"

Hearts pounded and feet ran as if they were on air headed toward the mountain and out of the forest as quickly as possible.

She yelled at me, "Eitan! Eitan! Come to me, Eitan!"

Her voice deepened and hissing screams filled the air.

"How dare you run from me, you ignorant child!"

Their eyes became the chilling gray and they resumed their hideous beastly forms as they hunted their prey.

Tucker certainly had more experience in running from things, but his current speed could have won Olympic races. He surpassed me by several feet.

"Look," he said as he motioned to an opening in the trees ahead. "It's a clearing! I can see the bottom of the mountain."

His pace never slowed.

As we fled past the last tree bordering the forest, we entered a meadow of tall dried grass that attempted to slow our every stride. Even though the mountain was in view, it was still a good mile, or more, through the meadow before we reached it. The creatures were closing in on us. We would never make it across the prairie in time. The sky filled with vultures and buzzards soaring with excitement. They were considerably loud and Tucker lost his focus. Concerned about the approaching predators, he looked back hoping to catch a glimpse of their distance, and stumbled to the ground. I reached him, and tried to help him up, but he was injured. There wasn't any time to assess his injuries and he spoke frantically.

"Ethan! Go- Leave me here!" he said.

"I'm not leaving you Tucker!" I exclaimed, and tried to raise him with little reciprocated help. "Get up!" I demanded.

"Ethan, run! It's ok, man. Maybe I can slow them down," Tucker said as he fought me off of him.

"Don't you understand? All is lost if you don't make it! Go!" he pleaded.

I was so torn, but I knew he was right. I had to make it to the mountain. Tears filled my eyes as I contemplated losing yet another friend. Fueled by grief and anger, I ran with every last ounce of energy possible. I heard the sound of the birds' cries as hundreds must have filled the sky above. Resembling the scream we heard from the crow before entering the forest, I heard a bird's soul-piercing scream as if it caught its prey. The hissing shrieks of breath now brushed against the back of my neck along with the beating wings of many birds. Knowing I would never outrun them, I felt the power in my legs fading. I gave in to the unknown and proceeded to glace back. Three white and hideous creatures lingered a short distance behind. The gnashing of their teeth and magnitude of their razor-like claws left me virtually frozen in shock.

"Ethan!"

I heard Tucker calling me, but couldn't see him anywhere. I closed my eyes in anticipation of being ripped to shreds. Suddenly, I was taken by surprise. Giant claws wrapped around my middle, and I heard the screeching of a hunter whom just caught his prey. I was lifted into the air at a high rate of speed. It wasn't until I realized I didn't feel any pain that I chose to open my eyes. The first face I saw was Tucker's, and I immediately wondered if I was dead also. He smiled, and I was more confused than ever. Upon second glance, I realized we were soaring through the air. I saw the three creatures in the prairie hundreds of feet below us. We soared above all the other birds, which began to look as small as ants. There was another loud and victorious shriek from the oversized and majestic eagle that held us tightly in his grasp.

"Is this bad?" I asked Tucker as I examined the size of the claws that embraced us.

"Not sure, but it's certainly better than the alternative," he said as he enjoyed the flight of victory.

We neared the mountaintop, and I realized how impossible it would have been for us to reach it on our own. It was very bright as we neared the top, and everything from the valley below looked like complete darkness. We circled the mountain a few times before the majestic bird gently placed us at the entrance to the cave atop the mountain. He stood tall and proud stretching his neck toward the sky as his wings spread wide. I noticed something glimmer in the light beneath his neck and partly hidden by his feathers. It was obvious he wanted me to investigate it. It was the third key! The eagle backed away from us and lowered himself to the ground bowing to me.

"Thank you," I said bowing my own head to acknowledge the eagle's wonderful favor.

"We made it," Tucker said, turning to the entrance of the cave.

I felt a great sense of accomplishment welling up inside of me, great joy knowing Tucker was still with me, and great anticipation of the things yet to come.

Chapter 20

It was amazing, and words simply couldn't accurately describe its beauty. The cave looked nothing like a cave on the inside. It was if I entered a secret room in a sanctified castle. The walls were lined with marble and diamonds. They contained incredibly ornate detail with gems of every kind. Their beauty continued across the vaulted ceiling etched with such significant detail. Everything in the room had a miraculous glow that lit the very core of one's soul. The treasure I had been sent to find was placed behind a royal purple curtain with the sides drawn back to reveal the beauty of the majestic wardrobe. It was separated into three sections, each of which contained a piece of the sacred armor.

I approached the wardrobe with humble admiration. A voice sounding as strong as a lion's roar, yet as gentle as the bleat of a lamb spoke to me.

"Welcome, Prince Eitan. We have expected you for quite some time now."

I stopped immediately where I stood and took a knee, bowing to the voice. I hadn't heard it before, but I inherently knew it was a member of the Kruathan people. Tucker followed my lead and also bowed down.

"Arise- Both of you. It is time for you to take back your rightful throne, Prince Eitan. Come, unlock the wardrobe so you may prepare for what is to come," the voice said with an underlying tone of excitement.

I removed the two keys and added them to the third. With great care, I placed them in the three keyholes that lined the center of the wardrobe. The wardrobe came to life and the keys were mystically turned, opening the doors. Light blinded me at first, and then I saw the majestic armor that was about to become mine. It was the first time I'd seen armor white in color.

"I crafted it with my own hands, and made it specifically with you in mind," the voice spoke with pride in his creation.

"I thought long and hard about each piece as I created it. The battle you are about to endure is not because of a choice *you* made. The choice was made for you, and with your best interests at heart. I knew you were worthy of armor that had never been used in battle; you need something unique and untouched by any darkness. We chose you, not *only* because of your lineage, but because we created you specifically for this purpose. From before you were born, we knew this day would come, and we have been planning and preparing the way for this very battle. You are destined to become our greatest warrior."

I examined the armor and became uncertain about many things. It was huge, and I'd never even come in contact with someone whom would've been able to fit into it properly. I remembered Aletheya, and even a man as large and tenacious as he, wouldn't have fit in it. I tried to pick up one of the gauntlets, and was stunned by the weight of it. How was I ever going to be able to wear this? If it didn't crush me from the weight, I certainly wasn't going to be able to battle in it. I wouldn't be able to move.

The breastplate magically arose and centered on my body.

"I thought about your heart as I created this piece. You are still young and have so much to learn, yet the things you have already been taught need protection. A righteous ruler must be wise in judgment and in the way he lives his life. He learns from the wisdom of others, and from his own faults and mistakes. He takes these lessons and buries them deep within his heart along with all the love, compassion, tenderness, and consideration for the ones he has been chosen to protect and defend."

It was so large I could barely see over it. Then, just as the voice had said, it formed to fit me. It was absolutely weightless. I caressed the chest and was very pleased by the smooth texture of it.

As my neck and mouth were covered next, the voice continued,

"Your neck connects the secrets of your heart to your mouth. Your words should always be chosen wisely. Listen more than you speak, and when you do speak, always speak the truth. You will learn lessons intended for you alone, and others would not understand even if you chose to share with them. Keep these secrets protected in your heart, and only share them when you are sure the moment is right."

The gauntlets formed around my hands, and the voice said, "Your hands are used for feeling and touching. It is with your hands you labor; you create with your hands."

I noticed the place where Haygon cut my palm back at the hideout, and the voice continued, "Your hands contain marks and scars to remind you of the places you have been, and the things you learned while you were there. Your hands have the power to project the great light inside of you that has magnificent power."

I wiggled my fingers and was impressed with how freely they still moved.

"Your legs carry you to the places you will go, they carry you into battle. Your legs are used for kneeling, when it is appropriate to kneel. Your feet guide the rest of your body to where it needs to go. Step carefully on new ground, and swiftly on ground that is not firm. Always find somewhere strong and solid plant your feet, especially when the ground around you is crumbling."

It suddenly occurred to me how I had been learning these things all along. I began to understand how each place I traveled taught me different lessons. I understood how they all had significance and how they were molding me all the while. The leg pieces and boots were now snug on my body.

The voice became solemn, "Each part of your body is delicate and precious, and each part works together to help the other. The mind is a miraculous mystery indeed. The mind provides a shelter for a tiny and unseen existence of the thing known as hope. A man can live several weeks without food, and a man can live several days without water. If a man were to try to survive without hope, he would instantly find it impossible. It is essential you fully understand what we promised unto you. We called you aside from your race to become unique and special. We created you specifically for a purpose that was never your own. Hope is your anchor, it gives you something to hold steadfast to. Hope is what drives your determination and motivation. Hope will sustain you until the end."

The armor seemed complete. It was weightless and conformed perfectly to my body. I turned and looked at Tucker. He appeared to be in a shocking trance when I spoke to him.

"So? How do I look?" I asked.

Tucker's face only displayed reverent adoration and respect, and his eyes blinked heavily to confirm his thoughts. Tucker carefully lowered his head, and descended to one knee.

"Tucker, what are you doing?" I asked.

His response was low and hard to understand at first.

"I'm not sure. I can't explain what I feel inside, but it feels like the right thing to do. I've never seen anything so majestic in all my life," he answered.

I smiled and spoke with appreciation, "Thank you, but you are being silly. Please get up…"

"Remember Prince Eitan, just as iron sharpens iron, so does one man sharpen another. You have many brothers whom need your guidance-"

The words interrupted by hissing sounds at the entrance. The creatures were quite large and blocked the light from outside.

"Impossible!" it hissed in between breaths.

"You belong to us! There is no armor that can protect you from the clinch of death!"

The beasts growled and spit with determination. Tucker slowly raised and moved out of the way. I caught a glimpse of my reflection and felt the power inside of me grow.

"It's the light, Eitan."

The voice spoke again, "The light we gave you has many powers. It is time you learn to use your power."

I was disgusted by watching the fangs on the beasts as they were covered by a slimy, slobbery substance resembling phlegm. It oozed from the edges of the mouth and dripped to cover the razor sharp claws. I became angry listening to the lies the beasts told me. I knew the truth and knew I shouldn't be afraid. My anger turned deeper with their threats against my family. They spoke of my birth mother and father and the things they would do to them. They glorified the horrific things they promised to do to Tucker, and Kallie. I was enraged by the repulsive beasts. My hands began to glow and I felt the armor absorbing the light from within me. I met eyes with the beast in the middle, and we both tried to get a glimpse of what was inside the other.

Without warning, the beast on the left leaped towards me. It caught me off guard and I pushed all my power to my left hand

and raised it in defense. After the bright light cleared, I noticed the beast was gone, and a shield remained in my hand. It was large and beautiful with great ornate details. On the front center was a glowing symbol. It was the same as the one on the back of my neck, and the same one on the cover of the book. It was a symbol I now associated with my very being. It brought me pride as I examined it.

The beasts became louder. The two turned and rubbed sides as they became one. It was much more intimidating and twice as large, but I was not afraid. My confidence grew every second and with every snarl the beasts made. I stood upright and firm, ready for attack. I lifted my shield and realized every piece of the armor was now brightly glowing. The beast lunged like a lion with claws primed for killing. I suppose my instincts intended for something else as my right hand jolted forward and a mighty sword emerged. I wasn't even sure it had struck the beast except for the small stain of blood on the tip. The beast screamed as it turned completely black and vanished into the air.

I heard the voice chuckle and speak with a humorous tone.

"Well Prince Eitan, *now.* Now your armor is complete. Congratulations. Know that we are watching you. Go. Defeat Lord Kiverus, take back your kingdom, and right every existence in every world."

I heard some stirring at the entrance and watched as Tucker climbed onto the back of the eagle.

"Come on, Ethan! Let's make you king of the worlds!" Tucker exclaimed as he motioned for me.

Chapter 21

His entire infant hand barely filled her palm. He was so quiet and peaceful; he was everything she hoped for. Her anxious spirit rarely allowed her to sleep with tranquility, but she loved the precious memories that occurred somewhere between dreams and reality. His memory was so much clearer when her eyes were closed. The only remembrance she had of Eitan was the short time she coddled him as a baby. Giana wondered if he would recognize her at all. Surely the sound of her voice would bring back the reminiscence of an earlier time. She always knew she could pinpoint him in any crowd if given the opportunity. Raeden often filled her with joy by telling stories of when Eitan was a small child. He had done well in protecting her precious gift. Raeden frequently assured her he did not leave Eitan before much thought was given to the situation. He made the right choice in leading Kiverus's disciples away from Eitan, and she knew it.

From the beginning, Giana knew it would be her sweet baby that would change everything. He was the one chosen to unite the nations and bring peace and righteousness back to Xaerdonia. She just never imagined it would happen the way it has. The Kruathans rarely chose to speak directly to either nation, and when they did, it was always through the willow tree. Giana remembered the day Eitan received his special gift from them. It was a perfect day, and everything seemed so right. It never occurred to her his gift was given to him because he would *need* it in order to survive the coming events.

The gift was given in the form of light; a light unlike any other. All Lathiaens and Candraens had a special light inside of them, but this was different. It wasn't the usual light inherited from generations before. It was a light that came directly from the Kruathans, and contained secrets that would be revealed to Eitan throughout his entire lifetime. This light gave the Kruathans the ability to speak directly to Eitan's heart; it empowered his very foundation. It is a light so unique that others can sense it just by being in his presence.

Both nations were immortal with only one provision. They could not allow the darkness to overcome them. It sounded quite simple, but recently became considerably more difficult. There was always a small amount of darkness tolerated in order for the guardians to accurately balance the worlds. Occasionally, the darkness beckoned to the hearts of particular ones who could not manage to withstand the temptation. Giana remembered how hard it was for her to remain strong after losing Eitan. Every ounce of strength was constantly at battle. Even after all this time, she still struggled. She had not given up yet though. Her hope remained in the promises of the Kruathans and the faith she would one day be reunited with her son.

Utter confusion filled every corner of every cell, and she forced her eyes to open. Thalesten was peacefully asleep. She reached through the bars and gently stroked his hair. He would have made such a great king. It saddened her to know his time was cut short, and he was never given the opportunity to prove how spectacular he could've been. Giana and her parents were the first Candraens ever allowed into Xaerdonia's temple. Thalesten was in the temple helping his father the first time she met him. She loved him from the moment their eyes first met. She watched quietly as he took the sands that belonged to each world and carefully tended to them. He led her by the hand and gently explained the importance of each one to her. It always puzzled her how the time of each world was contained within the sands and the way they needed to be precisely nurtured.

"My lady, listen," Raeden said, and motioned for her to come closer.

"Eitan found the armor. The warriors from both nations are uniting as we speak." Raeden whispered in order to contain his excitement.

Giana barely controlled her happiness. The disorder became louder and awakened Thalesten. He tried to make sense of the fuss going on around him when Giana whispered the good news in his ear. Cursing and louder commotion presented itself when several prison guards made their way toward Thalesten and Giana's cells.

Offering no explanation, Giana was taken by the arm and forcefully removed from her cell. It was the first time in fifteen years she set foot outside the door, but she knew it was not good.

She kicked, screamed, and even managed to bite one of the guards, but her efforts were useless. Raeden was angry enough to *melt* his way out of his cell if it were possible. Thalesten held his head high as they escorted him behind his opposing wife. If it weren't for the severity of the situation, he would've been quite impressed and almost amused with the resistance she gave them. He hoped the warriors preparing for battle had the slightest bit of her enthusiasm.

They were led into the boundaries of Xaerdonia. Giana stopped bickering when she realized where they were. Neither she nor Thalesten believed their eyes. The beautiful land they remembered turned to disgust within darkness, and the temple no longer glowed. Darkness covered everything. Giana's heart dampened with grief as her eyes followed the blackened water flowing from the temple to the tree. The trees all looked dead and starved. Even the majestic willow tree looked dehydrated and lifeless. It became harder to see as Giana and Thalesten were chained to the place specifically made for them.

"Do not fear, my love. He will be here soon. Do not let the darkness invade-"

Thalesten was forcefully slapped before he finished his statement. Giana regained determination while screaming at the guards to stop. How dare they touch her husband and in an ill manner!

"Silence!" a guard demanded as he violently struck Giana and momentarily paralyzed her.

Even though her eyes were swollen with tears, she saw his haunting gray eyes as they examined her. She wanted to spit in his face but her mouth was so dry she couldn't form the words to speak. His stench was overwhelming, and the nausea from her stomach reached her throat.

"It has been quite some time now, hasn't it?" Kiverus hissed loudly into her ear.

Thalesten struggled in his restraints as Kiverus took his long deathlike finger and stroked her cheek. Their eyes met and Kiverus intently centered on his brother. Thalesten had seen wickedness in his brother as far back as he remembered, but he never saw the extreme depths of it until this moment. Thalesten realized this was not the brother of his youth despite any remaining physical evidence.

Kiverus let out a hideous cry of laughter as his razor-like fingernails brought blood to Thalesten's arm. Thalesten groaned with intense pain.

"My power is much greater now, little brother," Kiverus said as he circled around them.

"Your precious little prince may have a special gift, but I too have been given a gift," Kiverus said with great confidence.

Kiverus loved how consuming his thoughts had been since he allowed the scorpion to join him. He was filled with passion and strength. His anger and intolerance of the Kruathans reached new levels, and he was ready to destroy everything. Knowing the extent of his powers, there was no doubt in his mind he should be looked at as an equal in their eyes. The time had come and he would, for once and for all, show them how wrong they were to regard him as weak and insignificant. He vowed never to cease tormenting the Kruathans. He would destroy everything they ever loved and would become their greatest enemy for all of eternity. He was sure they watched from their own world at that very moment.

He decided to test the strength of his brother's light.

"Why do you choose to be led by the Kruathans? Why do you and your people love them so much?" Kiverus taunted.

Thalesten remained silent.

"Do you not understand you are only a pawn in their eternal games? They don't care about you, or her," he said as he once again stroked Giana with his demon-like hands.

Thalesten fought within his constraints once again.

"Does it bother you to see the darkness touch the light? It should. You know my power is greater. You know I have the power to remove any existence of any light from your precious queen, if I so choose. If the Kruathans cared, they would have destroyed me from the beginning. Don't you think if they were as powerful as you believe, they could have abolished me? They didn't. They sent me here. They created me for a purpose just as they did your precious prince. They *wanted* me here. They sent me here to destroy everything they didn't have the heart to do themselves, including you. They are weak."

Kiverus came very close to Thalesten's face again.

He continued his hissing, "You don't know this, but I have lived with them once before. It's where I came from, and it is why I was sent here. They were afraid I was becoming too powerful; they knew I was going to be greater than they wanted. Yet, instead of destroying me, they sent me here. So that I would destroy their most beloved, and they could just watch without getting their own hands dirty. So prepare, brother of mine, prepare to watch as I destroy everything from this world and beyond."

Kiverus continued, "You may think you are too strong to allow the darkness in, but you are wrong. I am much stronger. It won't be long, and soon your little armies will be here. I'm sure they'll be led by your precious prince, but you will have a firsthand show of *my* greatness. And after I slaughter him, we'll see how strong you are."

Thalesten and Giana watched as Kiverus's army of disciples appeared from the darkest shadows. They were overwhelmed with the vast number, and as hard as they tried to not think about it, doubt began to creep into their minds.

Chapter 22

As if it wasn't unbelievable enough, I was soaring on an eagle. Every land we passed over looked as if it came straight out of a bizarre movie. Tucker remained speechless the majority of the flight. The eagle skimmed the surface of a large lake. As we flew over, I caught a glimpse of my reflection in the water. I saw the armor still on my body, but I still didn't *feel* it. It had become a part of me. We doubled our speed, and the eagle looked as though it was going to fly directly into a mountain. The light flashed green and we were in a new world. The eagle's scream filled the air and a rumble followed underneath us. The world was very dark with little light, yet it warmed me to be there. I was looking at the place that, until now, had only been real in my dreams. Through the distant darkness, there was a visible light.

I knew I was going to lead an army, but I never imagined it would be so large. We landed right in the middle of the crowd, and to my surprise, Caedmius was waiting to greet me. The cheering was so loud I couldn't hear him speak. Tucker and I dismounted from the eagle, and I showed my appreciation to the majestic bird. I didn't understand his language, but his eyes undoubtedly showed honor in helping me.

Caedmius's warriors seemed to be very controlled and in order, but there was much arguing and turmoil stirring between

the Lathiaens. "Who is in charge of the Lathiaens?" I asked
Caedmius.

He smiled as he answered. "You are."

I sighed realizing the answer to my question as he spoke it.
I heard two of them specifically discussing my parents and the fact
of whether or not they were alive.

A Candraen broke from his stance and with defending
words yelled, "It wasn't the Candraens that deceived everyone
and lied about the death of the Queen and King!"

The Lathiaen shoved him backwards as he yelled in return,
"We knew nothing other than what we were told! We were told
they died!"

His voice softened as his eyes met mine, and he
continued, "We were told that Prince Eitan also died. You've not
been the only ones hiding. We've been hiding as well, and all the
meanwhile hoping. Hoping that someone, somewhere, was
watching and waiting to redeem this once glorious land."

He walked over to me and continued to speak as he went
down to one knee, "We also considered the possibility all hope
was lost. But now, we can see that it is not."

While still bowing, he lifted his eyes and spoke with
reverence, "I am honored to serve you, Prince Eitan. I am
honored to fight beside you while you regain all that belongs to
you. Your age is insignificant to the strength and power you
display with the light inhabiting you. The only obvious conclusion

is you are completely extraordinary, and destined for eternal greatness among all our people."

Silence was contagious among the crowd. I surveyed the mighty warriors that stood before me. They were some of the most tenacious beings I'd encountered. Yet, despite their substantial build, their faces disclosed their inner fears and doubt. How I could possibly change their assumptions? I noticed a small and feeble lizard sitting by a fire and remembered the courage he portrayed.

Caedmius placed his hand on my back as he spoke, "They are much like you. Unsure of many things, but the light inside of them calls them to greatness. They know there is something more than what they have witnessed. They know a greater light is calling them to a greater destiny. You were chosen to give them a greater purpose, to magnify their hope and faith, to give them a reason to carry on, and to give them an existence worth fighting for."

I was unsure of what I should to say to them and unclear of the qualities I needed in order to prove myself a worthy leader. Once again, I caught an unexpected glimpse of myself through the reflection of a Candraen shield.

"When exactly did the ordinary become extraordinary?" I mumbled to myself.

Somewhere under the layers of armor, I saw the same boy that wanted more than anything to impress those around him. I saw the boy completely taken by a beautiful girl and would walk to the ends of the world for her. A boy trying to survive the transformation from child to man by confronting the most conceited bully in town. I saw the boy who was so consumed within his own world that the very notion of other worlds depending on him was entirely unfathomable.

My thoughts became words, "I've had some pretty unbelievable dreams over the past few months. I can honestly say *never* in my wildest dreams did I expect to be standing in the middle of the greatest army known to any world and about to lead them into an epic battle determining the fate of every being near and far. I'm not sure *why* I was chosen for this task. I'm obviously not trained and skilled like the rest of you, and I certainly don't have your physique. Yet I was chosen. I was given a light that holds special gifts; a light never seen by any world. I was told I was created for this purpose, and I would be the one to rectify this once beautiful land. I've gone through many trials over the last few days. My heart has ached, been torn, and frightened. It has longed to see loved ones. It has made new friendships-only to lose them, and it has been pulled and stretched in many directions. Darkness sought to steal the light inside of me with every move I've made. Darkness tried to befriend me, tempt me, call to me-with the sole intention to kill me. I've met many creatures, and beings, and learned how the darkness has stolen things from their lives, and from the lives of the ones they love. The darkness isn't always obvious. It creeps, and it hunts like a lion searching for prey. It quickly consumes the weak, and slowly plagues the wiser and stronger. The darkness brings an unbearable weight that seems impossible to overcome, and it only needs a tiny entrance into our hearts.

The fact is, the darkness has infected all the worlds, and has almost completely taken over Xaerdonia. We only have two choices. We can either choose to ignore it and hide from it, or we can choose to stand and fight against it. We may be standing in the pit of utter darkness at this very moment, but we can still fight. We can use the light within each of us and leave the darkness without a place to stand.

There has been a great divide between the Lathiaens and the Candraens. The hurt and anger you feel toward one another, is hindering you from becoming all you were meant to be. The Kruathans gave all of us special powers, not just me. They gave us these powers in order to be guardians over all the worlds. It is our responsibility, our duty, our honor, to fulfill these wishes. Now, I can't force you to forgive, and I can't force you to change your dispositions. I can ask that you look around. Right now," I pointed around to each of them, "look around. We are all here for the same purpose, we all care, and we all know it is our commission to succeed in this purpose. Whether or not you realize it, we *are* all brothers."

I placed my arm around Tucker, and continued, "All of us. It isn't our blood, our race, or even our world that unites us. It's the fact you are willing to sacrifice yourself for the one standing next to you in order to justify what is right. Listen closely, dear brothers…" absolute silence filled the air as they held their breath in anticipation, "…Can you hear it? Listen with your heart, and listen with the light you hold deep inside. You hear the sound of the ones that allowed the darkness to overtake them. They beg you to hold on, to place your focus where it should be, to hear their pleas, and to be strong where they were weak. If we do not join together now, we will be destroyed one by one, just as they were. As individuals we are strong, but together-we are insurmountable!"

The Lathiaen walked over to the Candraen he had shoved, and I wondered if my words had any influence at all. All doubt melted as he extended his hand to his Candraen brother. They embraced each other, as others did the same. The feeling of unity quickly spread throughout the entire crowd, and I knew it was time. I knew they were ready to stand against the darkness. My heart pounded with anticipation of what was to come.

A voice spoke and I was sure I was the only one who heard it. "Well done, Prince Eitan. You will lead this mighty army into the land that has no light. Know we are with you, we will guide you, and we will be fighting beside you even though you won't see us. We will always be with you, even until the ends of all the worlds."

Chapter 23

Thalesten begged Giana to not give in, but it wasn't until she heard the screaming sound from above that she regained her focus. The wind blew fiercely with every beat of the eagle's wings. Lord Kiverus called for his disciples and warned them to prepare for battle. Kiverus paced on the marble altar as his disciples surrounded and awaited his commands. The eagle let out a final cry as he disappeared up and beyond the dark clouds. Everything remained motionless and intense. Kiverus listened closely. He was substantially controlled although his eyes revealed his uncertainty as they frantically searched the land looking for any movement. A loud rumble of thunder shook the very ground beneath the altar. Kiverus had been surrounded by darkness for so long that the light protruding from the top of the hill hurt his eyes. Each Lathiaen and Candraen had a glowing veranum displaying on their hands.

"You come with your precious little lights, but as you can see," Kiverus continued as he raised the hand of one of his disciples, "I have the power to stomp out your disgusting display."

The disciple's veranum had a mystic black shadow where the light used to be.

The army continued to fill the darkness with a small amount of light, and Lord Kiverus laughed.

"Is that it? Is that all? You look like a tiny firefly attempting to light the entire world. Where is this mighty Prince Eitan that leads you? Has he realized he is too weak?"

"Not quite, Kiverus!" I said as I appeared on a small hill to the left of his many disciples.

Lord Kiverus let out a blood-curling forced laughter as he spoke, "Is that all? You aren't even large for a child. This is what the Kruathans decided they would send? To defeat me?" His laughter continued, "Kill them all!"

Kiverus's disciples carried their own darkened armor and charged toward the waiting army. I'd never witnessed a war first hand, but it looked exactly how I would've imagined it. There was clashing of swords and shields with sweat and effort flourishing among the warriors. The back of my neck began to burn, and the glowing light surrounded me. Unable to tell if one side or the other was gaining advantage, Kiverus's hallow eyes met mine as he attempted to stare into my soul. I refused to allow him to penetrate any part of my mind, and ran full force to the front of the battle line. I stabbed numerous disciples, yet they were untouched. I was confused. How were we to defeat his army of disciples if our weapons had no more effect on them than they would on a ghost? Their darkened bodies dissolved like a mystic shadow and then reappeared unaffected.

Caedmius let out a horrific scream of agony as one of the disciples shoved their sword into his arm leaving a trace of darkness behind. It reminded me of what I saw the scorpion do to

Ceana's leg when she was pregnant. Caedmius fell to the ground in anguish as another Candraen attempted to console him. The battle wasn't going the way I had hoped. More and more injured Candraen and Lathiaen warriors fell to the ground. Their veranums were fading, and some had lost all light. Circling around, I heard the haunting laughter once again.

"Little Prince Eitan! Continue to look around, you *are* defeated! Surrender to me now and save your followers from further torture and torment!" Kiverus shouted above the crowd.

I raised my sword to indicate I would not bow down before him. As I did, there was a sharp stabbing in my side. I saw the hollow eyes of a disciple as he hissed the words, "I will win, either by your death or your surrendering."

I touched the painful area in my side only to find what should have been blood, looked like oil leaking from my wound. I lost my breath as I hit the ground. The commotion surrounded me, but I couldn't find the strength to open my eyes. My head was lifted off the ground and I heard Tucker's voice filled with tears.

"Ethan! Wake up Ethan!" he said as he shook me.

I choked as I tried to speak. I saw a dim vision of Tucker decked out in full armor as he tried to bring me back to consciousness.

"Ethan! You can't give up! What are you doing? If you let the darkness win, all is lost! Not just this world, but *our* world...all the worlds!"

The shaking became violent as his pleas turned to tear-filled screams, "Ethan! Please!"

I tried harder to open my eyes and saw my mother and father still restrained at the altar. Kiverus screamed into their faces, but I was unable to hear what he said. He turned and pointed into the crowd of warriors and then Giana screamed, "Father! No!"

She focused on Caedmius struggling to fight with every last ounce of strength. *Father?* It occurred to me at that moment, Caedmius was my grandfather. I couldn't believe I didn't see it before, but it all made sense now.

My light faded as Caedmius' image became clearer. It was as if I was entering a dream, but I was able to block out all other noise and concentrate solely on his voice.

"Eitan! Why are you giving up? You were destined for this very moment, for this very battle. This is what you were created for. Don't let the darkness into your soul. Don't let him win! You have the power inside of you to chose, don't you understand?"

Caedmius petitioned the very core of my soul, but I couldn't. For the first time since I'd left home, the weakness was beyond my control.

Suddenly, my eyes opened wide with the resonant sound of a majestic bird's call. He flew high above us as he attempted to pull back the clouds of darkness to reveal a small ray of light. I was able to lift my head and see Tucker with his eyes still full of fright and tears. Caedmius slowly made his way over to me, and with every inch I felt my strength coming back.

"Ethan, Look," Tucker said as he lifted my hand to my face.

The armor had a slight shimmer to it that wasn't there before. I felt my neck getting warmer, but this time, I felt it throughout my whole body.

"Yes, Eitan! You see. You need to let go of your doubts and just believe," Caedmius said with pride as his own body began to lose the darkness that recently invaded it.

I gained more strength with every breath, and Tucker held out his hand to help me up. Caedmius stood front and center with a smile. His veranum was glowing so brightly it should have been blinding us both. I examined his arm and was surprised the darkness was completely gone.

"It is because of you," he said as he rubbed his once wounded limb.

"You see, my sweet grandchild, it is because of your light, that my light was able to shine once again. The light of a candle is magnificent to shine alone, but when joined with another candle, shines even brighter and more powerful."

Caedmius continued, "Now, the rest of your people need you."

There were fading Candraen and Lathiaen warriors all around me. Kiverus stood frozen on his altar. One of my Candraen brothers fell to the ground beside me. My armor shimmered with magnificent light now. As his hand lifted toward me, I reached down and firmly grabbed his hand in return. His eyes became full, and as he took a deep breath of air, I lifted him from the ground. His veranum shone as brightly as Caedmius'. I proceeded to help others around me while spreading the word about the strength in their joined light, and to help one another. The nearby disciples vanished into the light and didn't return. One by one, they either ran or were consumed by the surrounding light. The eagle screeched as he struggled with a layer of clouds, but managed to reveal a large ray of light that shone directly on our glorious army of warriors.

Kiverus cringed at the site, and was tormented by its brightness. My path was made clear and I walked proudly toward him.

"Kiverus! I am Eitan, Prince of Light, and Prince of Xaerdonia! You came to destroy all we know, but you have failed miserably. You brought your darkness with you, and for a moment, we allowed it to live amongst us. But now, and for no longer will it be allowed here! You were allowed to remain in Xaerdonia with hopes that someone, or something would be able to shine their light into your darkness, but it was a hopeless wish. You deceived your very brothers; you stole their souls and left them to reside alone in your dark world."

I lifted my sword and walked confidently closer, saying, "You held the righteous guardians captive, and stole the lives of others. I may have been gone for the last fifteen years, but I am here now! I understand what you are and where you have come from! I am here to destroy you the way you have intended to destroy us!"

He cowered from the light surrounding him. I stood over him with my sword raised. He covered his face with his hands as he prepared for the ultimate ending. With every bit of might inside of me, I allowed my sword to come flying down with the greatest of force. It struck the ground of the altar and created a large crevice. I had one foot placed firmly on each side of the chasm. He looked amused that the sword missed him- not realizing it was never my intention to strike him. His euphoria only lasted seconds as he was entirely consumed by the light that beamed up from the hole. He howled with anguish as his body transposed into a vanishing shadow. Light now filled all of Xaerdonia, and we all watched as the remains of his soul were sucked into the lighted hole before it closed around him. There was a great roll of thunder and the restraints that held Thalesten and Giana were broken. Every cell within the prison burst wide open and all were free. My heart leapt for joy as I knew we succeeded.

Giana held my face in her hands as her eyes filled with tears.

"My son. My precious son," she said as she wrapped her arms around me tightly. "You will never know how much I've missed you."

The light filled the land almost as quickly as the cheering from the celebrating warriors. Everything felt as though it would be okay.

Chapter 24

The breeze certainly felt different this time. In fact, the whole atmosphere was different this time- it felt real and unlike any dream. I closed my eyes and inhaled the refreshing air as if it were the first time I'd ever breathed. My father and mother waited for me in the temple. I contently observed the water flowing from the temple into the garden of trees. They looked as I always envisioned them, full of life. The water was no longer black and stained with darkness. It wasn't completely pure yet, but it would be soon. The wind picked up speed and blew the leaves of the willow tree across my face.

"Eitan. Eitan, can you hear us?"

"I can hear you," I answered.

The voice returned, "Sweet Eitan, you have grown so much since we first brought you here."

I felt a branch gently cross my cheek, and they wrapped around me. They pulled me closer to the massive trunk.

I heard the voice chuckle, saying, "We are so proud of you. You have finished your task victoriously, and have learned much along the way." The branches released me slightly. "We also sense not all is right for you. What bothers you?"

I answered with a heavy heart, "I know my responsibilities and duties are of greatest importance here, and although it may sound completely childish, I miss my home."

The voice was very soft as it spoke, "Prince Eitan. It is the name we gave to you. It is a name that holds magnificent honor. You are correct, you have many responsibilities here, but they do not all have to be fulfilled immediately."

The water below the tree began to ripple and I saw the faces of my mom and dad back home. I saw Kallie, and as the wind blew I caught a glimpse of her wonderful scent. I saw Tucker, and it wasn't until I felt his hand on my shoulder I realized it was his actual reflection I was looking at.

"They are waiting for you," Tucker said.

"I'll be right there, just another minute," I replied.

Tucker nodded and made his way back to the temple.

The voice continued, "Sweet prince, we knew you left a part of your heart at home. The Candraens and Lathiaens are at peace with each other, but they still need a leader. I think this is a task your father would be honored to fulfill at this time if it is all right with you."

My heart raced at the thought of being able to return home.

"You have been given many powers, and you will retain these powers no matter where you are. They have become a part of you. We will always be here to guide you in whatever adventures you seek out, and when you dream, listen for us. Your veranum will stay with you also, but it will remain invisible while you are in other worlds unless it is touched by a fellow Candraen or Lathiaen."

The ripples ceased and from the corner of my eye, I saw my father standing at the temple entrance. I touched the truck of the tree, said *"goodbye,"* and walked excitedly toward the temple.

"Is everything all right?" Lord Thalesten asked.

"Yeah, just saying goodbye," I replied.

"Goodbye? Where are you going?" he asked.

"Hopefully home," I said as his face became saddened. "I mean...I know this is my home also. It's just-"

"I understand," he interrupted. "It's all right as long as you come to visit," he said with an understanding smile.

Giana had been listening.

"Excuse me, but there is still one problem that remains," she said.

I was confused as we followed her into the temple. There was a large fountain with several different elements being suspended above it.

"The time holders," Lord Thalesten whispered. "I forgot," he said as he pointed out an empty space. Kiverus destroyed the time holder belonging to the world you have called home."

They looked very familiar and it took me a moment to remember where I had seen their unique shape before. Then I remembered, the necklace given to me in my dream. I pulled it out and handed it to my father.

"Will this work as a replacement?" I asked.

"Where did you get this?" he asked with amazement.

"Believe it or not, it was given to me by a beautiful woman in a dream I had," I answered.

He looked disappointed as he took it.

"It would work just fine except for one problem. It doesn't have any sand," he said.

"Sand?" I asked.

"Yes, it works as an endless hourglass, but still needs the sand in order to function properly. I'm sorry. Without it, your world can not continue," he replied.

Tucker seemed distraught, saying, "Funny how some worlds seem to have too much sand and others not enough, huh?"

"That's it, Tucker!" I exclaimed.

"What's it?" he asked.

I pulled out the tiny pouch the sand princess gave me.

"She said I would know when to use this, and I suppose now is as good of time as any," I said.

I opened the strings to the pouch, and the sand penetrated through the walls of the time holder and behaved as if it were always there. Lord Thalesten gently grasped the time holder and positioned it in the proper place. It began to spin in place, and like a sandstorm out of control, sand appeared all around us. I could see visions of the sand princess, Harent, and even Haygon in the midst of the sand. They were all transformed back to the way they were before the curse. I knew in my heart their world was set right, and joyfully anticipated the day I would journey back to visit them also.

A tall and sturdy man entered the room. He looked familiar but I wasn't sure from where. He spoke with a deep and enchanting voice.

"I guess you aren't as scrawny as I thought you'd be after all," he said.

I wasn't sure if I should be offended or not.

Lord Thalesten burst out in laughter, saying, "Eitan, this is Raeden. He was your guardian for many years, and we owe him much gratitude."

I reached out my hand in order to greet him, but was answered with yet another bear hugging squeeze.

"I've waited a long time to see you rise to your full potential. I knew you had it in you, kid," he said.

His pat on my back nearly made me lose my footing. "Thanks…I think," I said.

"Well Eitan, are you ready to return home? I think you have a special young lady who will be excited to see you," Lord Thalesten said as he winked at Raeden.

"Yes. I'm sure she will be thrilled," Raeden replied.

I looked at Tucker and laughed at his apprehension about traveling.

"Come on, Chicken, we need to get home," I said.

"I just hope there *is* some of your mom's chicken when we get there!" Tucker replied.

I took once last glance as Giana pressed her lips and blew me a kiss, "Take care, my sweet boy."

"I'll be watching you," said Raeden as he motioned two fingers from his eyes to mine.

Lord Thalesten nodded his head, "Return soon. We love you, Son."

I closed my eyes only to see a bright green flash and felt Tucker's grip tighten.

We were home.

"Yes! Yes! Yes!" Tucker screamed as he literally fell down and touched the ground with his cheek.

"We made it Ethan! Yes! We're home!" he exclaimed.

I was every bit on the inside as excited as he was on the outside.

"Come on, man," Tucker said as we started down the sidewalk home.

The sound of normality surrounded us and it was wonderful. Small pieces of trash remained on Dane's front lawn as evidence a party existed.

"Wow. What a night, huh?" I asked Tucker as we walked by.

"Yeah, one heck of a-"

He was interrupted by the most beautiful sound in the world, Kallie.

"Ethan!"

I heard her scream as she came running toward us. She caught her breath as she reached us.

"You found him!" she exclaimed with excitement.

"Huh?" I asked.

"Tucker! You found Tucker!"

"Oh yeah, I did. I, uh...I found Tucker back at the school," I stuttered.

"I've been so worried about you," she said.

She was almost in tears which confused me.

"Worried about *me*? Why would you be worried about-"

"*Hush*," she whispered as she leaned forward and kissed me with great passion.

I tightened my grip around her waist almost lifting her into the air.

Tucker was almost embarrassed, but was enjoying the moment Ethan waited so long to have. He thought about sneaking past and heading home when something caught his eye. It was the back of Ethan's neck. Kallie was fervidly running her hands through Ethan's hair as they kissed and it appeared to be making his veranum glow. Then, Tucker realized it wasn't at all what he thought. It was Ethan making Kallie's veranum glow.

Tucker's mouth practically hit the ground as he saw the bright blue moon appearing more intensely on her hand. Kallie's attention was caught by the blue light, and her eyes met Tucker's as she continued her kiss. She cautiously moved her hand lower to lessen the glow, and her eyes pleaded with him to not say anything about her secret. Tucker smiled and made the motion across his lips as if to say they were sealed.

Ethan held her hand on the walk home and she made sure it stayed behind his back. Most of the shimmering markings had disappeared completely by the time they reached the house.

Screaming and squealing came from inside of Ethan's house right before Tucker's mom came running through the door and grabbed him in her arms. His dad followed closely behind, and they embraced the bond of their family for several moments. His mother was crying for him to please never scare her that way again. Tucker assured them both it wasn't his intention to scare them, and he loved them very much.

I hugged my own mother and was glad to be home. Kallie looked uncomfortable with the family reunions that were taking place. I wished I could heal that part of her heart, but let her go home knowing she needed some time alone.

Tucker yelled back from his front lawn,

"Hey! Ethan! Don't forget to work on that science project, man! Remember, time waits for no man, and it's due on Monday!" I waved and walked into my house. I loved knowing I was home. I loved the feeling of butterflies in my stomach from the kiss I just had. I loved knowing I was anything but ordinary, and I didn't need to prove anything to anyone, anymore.

Chapter 25

It was great to be able to stretch out in my own bed, my own room. It was only seconds before I was in a deep sleep. I should have known better than to think I'd go to sleep without dreaming about *something*. For once, I was a bystander in my own dream.

There was a little girl starring deep into my eyes. She must have been around four years old, and had the most beautiful green eyes. I nearly lost myself in her long lashes as she blinked them, they seemed so familiar. A man walked in the room, but I only saw him from behind. He sat down in the floor as she smiled and ran to him.

She spoke sweetly, "Daddy,"

He held his hand out to help balance her and I saw the familiar blue moon appear on her tiny hand. As he lifted her into his lap, he sang a slumbering lullaby to her. Just as she closed her eyes he whispered, "Sweet Kallie of mine, I hope you know how much Daddy loves you. I have so much to teach you."

"Ray. Ray. There you are," Anna said, appearing in the doorway looking beautiful and carefree.

"I was just tucking Kallie in bed," he replied. "I'll be right there, my love."

He placed her gently in her bed and the glow from both of them was gone.

I followed Ray out of the room, but I entered a different time. Kallie was about a year older.

"Daddy, tell me another story," Kallie said as she climbed into his lap.

"Kallie sweetheart, listen to me. These aren't all make-believe stories, and I need you to try to understand them." His heart softened as he looked into her eyes.

"I understand, Daddy. Tell me more about the prince," she begged.

"Well, where were we last? I think we left our prince in trouble, didn't we?"

Kallie nodded her head, "Yes he is getting in big trouble, and we were about to help him,"

"That's right, Baby," he said as he placed his hand on hers and a faint glow appeared. "We need to help the prince, always. Daddy may not always be here, and it will be *your* turn to help the prince all by yourself."

He kissed her on the forehead and continued his story.

There was a bright flash, and I was again in a different time and place. This time, Kallie was several years older. She was lying in her bed crying uncontrollably. Her dad stood in the doorway with tears filled in his own eyes. He moved to the edge of her bed trying to reason with her. "Kallie, sweetheart, I know you don't understand, but I need you to be my big princess and be strong right now."

"Daddy, I wanna go with you! Why can't I go this time? You've let me go before!" she pleaded.

"Kallie, it's different this time. I'm not going on a journey for fun and fantasy. It's time, Baby. Don't you remember me telling you there would come a time?" he said as he broke both their hearts.

"I want to go visit uncle Cayne, can I stay with him until you get back?" she asked.

"No, Sweetheart. You can't travel like that anymore. Don't you understand? Your mother doesn't know anything about this. In order to protect Mommy and keep her safe, it has to be our secret. Okay, Baby?"

Kallie began to cry harder, and he attempted one last time to reason with her.

"Baby girl, please listen. I have to go. If I stay, I am putting everyone in danger! I need you to remember the stories I've told you, remember the places we have been, and remember that they are real. I need you to look for the prince. He's here, and when you find him, you'll know. Remember that he will need your help. It is what you and I have been chosen to do. You'll always be my sweet princess, and I will come back to you and Mommy. I love you, please don't ever forget this!"

He left her sitting on the bed as he quickly went into the closet and closed the door behind him. A flash of light came from under the door, and Kallie began screaming for her daddy. Anna came running into the room trying to comfort her child, without a clue of what happened.

The next several images flashed quickly in my dream, but I remembered seeing Kallie through different phases of my life. She was always close by, even if she didn't realize it, she was. I saw the last night we were together before everything changed. I realized why she was so sensitive about her father and his disappearance. I saw flashes of Kallie and her uncle Cayne. Flashes of Liora and how she continued to guide me, and help me. I had the overwhelming feeling that Kallie had been with me all along. She was helping me just as she was asked.

I was awakened by loud giggling and laughter coming from downstairs. My mother was cooking something wonderful for breakfast. I grabbed a shirt that was sitting on the edge of my dresser and looked at myself in the mirror before I put it on. I may not have changed much physically in the last few days, but there was certainly a visible change. Personally, I thought I looked complete in the maturity department. Okay, well, maybe I had a little more maturing to do, but I was more than willing to take on any challenges before me.

My presence was undetected as I leaned against the kitchen doorway. I watched my mother sharing her cooking secrets with Kallie. Anna came around the corner with a towel and drying her hands as she laughed.

"Sherri, this soap is simply amazing! My hands have never felt this soft!"

My mom replied, "I'm not sure about the soap, but this fruit that Kallie brought over is exquisite!"

She carefully sliced a strange little purple fruit I'd only seen one other time in my life.

She continued, "This will make a wonderful pie! I hope you and Kallie will join us for dinner tonight. I believe the Tuckers are going to be here as well. It's been a long time since we've had a full house. It will be splendid company."

I coughed gently to make my presence known. Kallie blushed as our eyes met, which made me remember our kiss and the fact I so desperately wanted more.

"Good morning, Sweetheart," my mom said. She walked over and roughed up my hair even further.

"Kallie and Anna brought some amazing fruit over this morning. You should try some."

I couldn't take my eyes off of Kallie.

"It's really amazing, Ethan," she said as she handed me the purple fruit.

"Yeah, she is," I said without even thinking.

Anna giggled slightly and tried to maintain a conversation with my mom ignoring the fact I was embarrassing myself. Kallie was washing some dishes when she dropped a glass shattering it. It startled everyone. My mom rushed over and asked if she was all right, but Kallie just stared out the window as she answered.

"Daddy?"

My mom was confused by Kallie's response, "What…"

"Daddy!" Kallie screamed this time. She took off out the door and across the lawn.

"Daddy?" repeated Anna as she cautiously walked to the window.

She couldn't believe her eyes. She watched as Kallie was lifted into the air by the man she'd never forget. It *was* him. Tears fell uncontrollably from her eyes and she walked unsteadily outside. Ray saw Anna and he placed Kallie back on the ground as he walked quickly to meet Anna.

"Ray?"

Anna barely got the words out before she fell completely limp.

He caught her and held her in his arms, saying, "It's me Baby. I'm home."

I stood at the door with my mom as we watched the reunion.

"Well, that's just beautiful. I love happy endings," she said, acting as though she wanted to clap her hands at the end of a movie.

"I suppose I'll set one more place for dinner tonight."

As Ray turned his face, I was able to see my suspicions were correct. It was Raeden, my faithful guardian.

Epilogue

It was Monday morning, which meant it was time to go to school. The doorbell rang a little early, and I opened the door to find Kallie standing there.

"Good morning. Are you ready?" she asked.

"Ready for what exactly?" I asked in return.

"Ready to walk your girlfriend to school," she blushed and giggled.

Tucker came walking up the sidewalk.

"Are we going to make it a trio this morning, Bro?" he asked.

I grabbed my bag and headed out the door. The conversation was exciting that morning, and none of us could quit talking. When we reached the school, Shelby interrupted us and brought us back to current events.

"Hey Kallie, I just wanted to apologize for my attitude Friday night," Shelby said.

She still looked me up and down, but not with as much objection as usual.

"He's all right with us. As long as he treats you like a princess, he can be your prince," said Shelby.

She gave Kallie a hug, and then winked at me as she walked away with Megan. It felt odd, but great to be standing proudly next to Kallie as her boyfriend. And then it happened.

"Moron!"

It was the unmistakable voice of Dane Ivey approaching quickly behind us. Before we could even turn around, Tucker was pushed to the ground.

"You got jokes do you?" Dane demanded.

I had enough. With one hard thrust, I pushed Dane back several feet and was ready for what had been building for years. The rage built in his eyes, but he was caught off guard by Tucker.

He jumped in front of us, placed both his hands on my chest, and said, "Thanks, Bro. But I got this one."

I was confused as he winked and turned to face Dane.

"So you think you're a superhero without your glasses or something?" Dane taunted Tucker.

With three simple words, and a deep breath, "Something like that," Tucker slammed one hard punch right into Dane's jaw knocking him out cold. The few bystanders stood motionless as Dane's limp body crumpled to the ground.

People began to cheer and congratulate Tucker. Coach Arnold walked right through the middle of the crowd and stared at Tucker for a moment before he spoke.

"Hey, kid," he said as he examined Tucker's physique.

"How come I ain't got ya on any of my teams? Come see me sometime, we need to talk," he said smirking at Dane's body as he walked away without remorse.

I kissed Kallie before she went to her first class. Still amazed over Tucker's incredible knockout I had to ask,

"So, Tuck, where exactly did *that* come from?"

"What? The punch?" Tucker asked.

"Yeah. *The punch*. I didn't know you had it in you," I replied.

Tucker laughed as he kiddingly punched my arm, "Whatcha mean, hero boy? You didn't think I learned anything while we were out gallivanting around saving the world?"

"I always knew you had it in you," I replied.

Our conversation continued as we finished at our lockers. Tucker's hand caressed the dent on his locker and then shuttered at the thought. The locker on the other side of him slammed and startled us both.

"I'm sorry," said a beautiful voice to Tucker. "I didn't mean to startle you."

Tucker turned to look at her as she continued, "Hi. My name is Abigeal. I'm new, and this is my first day here."

She grabbed his hand, "I'd hoped you would show me around?"

Tucker looked at me with pure bliss. I understood exactly how he felt.

I wasn't sure what the future held, but as far as I could see...it was going to be extraordinary!